The Other Side
Of Rain

by

Jud Scheaf

Infinity Publishing

Copyright © 2001 by Jud Scheaf

ISBN 0-7414-0564-4

Published by:

Infinity Publishing.com
519 West Lancaster Avenue
Haverford, PA 19041-1413
Info@buybooksontheweb.com
www.buybooksontheweb.com
Toll-free (877) BUY BOOK
Local Phone (610) 520-2500
Fax (610) 519-0261

Printed in the United States of America

Printed on Recycled Paper

Published February-2001

Delaware Author

Donated by

the author

To the only woman I ever truly loved.

"Security is mostly a superstition. It does not exist in nature ... Life is either a daring adventure or nothing."

-Helen Keller

Chapter 1

James Allen Hempstead sat in an over-stuffed leather chair and stared intently at the pearl-handled revolver sitting on the table next to him. It was lying just next to a glass spilling over with Jack Daniel's. Hempstead's wife and son had been asleep for hours, but he still carried the energy from the day and it would not allow him to join them. And so he sat alone with his hands sweating and his eyes no longer relaying images of the reality about him. Lost in concentration over the resting gun, he studied the sleek and metallic contours of the implement until he knew it intimately.

It was always the same when Jim Hempstead got this way. He wondered whether he would feel the pain as the bullet ripped his brain apart, or the electricity as it burned his body, or the carbon monoxide as it took his life. He wished that there would be no pain, just the immediate gratification from the ultimate release. God, it would make it all worthwhile if he could just live for that split second when it all came rushing out of him and his mind went empty.

It had been some time ago that Jim Hempstead stopped blaming everyone else for his depression and reluctantly accepted his lot in life. Indeed, he could just as easily change the color of his brown eyes as escape from the stultifying and ubiquitous cloud that existed about him.

Snapping back from his warped meditation, Hempstead caught himself staring at the weapon and he wondered for how long he had withdrawn to his secret dimension. The ice cubes in his glass had not completely melted so it could not have been that long --not compared to the empty years he had accumulated along the way.

He drank the frigid whiskey in three quick gulps before quietly creeping up the stairs and into his son's room. Careful not to awaken the boy, he put the toy gun back in the plastic holster hanging over a bedpost where it belonged. Jim Hempstead desperately needed some rest: he had to be in court very early in the morning.

Hempstead had been before a jury many times before. His appearance was just as important as his message. He wore a navy-blue suit, a crisp white shirt, and a conservative red tie. His polished black shoes and neatly trimmed hair were a testament to his concern for detail.

Hempstead was not a tall man, but neither was he small. He had dark wavy hair and a clean-shaven face with nothing unusual about it other than its youthful features. Had it not been for his presence, one might never suspect that he had endured forty-two years on the earth. Hempstead had a confidence about him that could only come from experience and it showed.

As he stepped up to deliver his closing argument on behalf of the McDonald's Corporation, Jim Hempstead appeared poised and comfortable. He was about to pour his heart and passion into an argument concerning whether the sauce that a McDonald's franchisee used on its Big Mac comported with the company's secret recipe. He had prepared for years for this moment and the stakes were high. The slightest deviation in the recipe would cost the franchisee the right to display the golden arches.

Hempstead had built his case around a theme and it was time to sell it to the jurors and convince them about the virtues of the special sauce. He went into detail concerning the ingredients of the secret recipe and how the derelict franchisee had changed it. He summarized the expert testimony and the consumer survey evidence that revealed the evils of the bad sauce. He had been talking for well over an hour before he finally neared the end of his argument.

"It's been a long two weeks and I want to conclude by king you again for your valued service to the public.

2

You have heard the testimony and have had the chance to evaluate for yourselves the credibility of the witnesses. This case comes down to one critical issue: does each and every person here and across the country who pulls into a McDonald's drive-thru window, or brings his family into one of its restaurants, have a right to expect that a Big Mac will taste like a Big Mac? Of course they do. That is what the golden arches are all about. When a person goes into a McDonald's he or she knows what to expect." He paused and stepped from behind the wooden podium walking up to the jury box so that he was able to place his hands on the railing directly in front of his audience. Properly positioned, he lowered his voice and looked each of them in the eyes.

"Ladies and Gentlemen, you have the power to tell this franchisee that enough is enough. You have the power, and indeed the obligation, to send a message, and send it loud and clear. Tell this franchisee and each and every franchisee across the country that they can not change the secret recipe or anything else that you've come to know and love from McDonald's. I know that you will do the right thing. Thank you."

Hempstead sat down, relaxed and listened as the judge gave the jury instructions. It was his favorite part of any case. He had done everything he possibly could have done to win. He had taken countless depositions. He had written and responded to many briefs. He had spent months getting ready for trial. But everything was out of his hands as the jury went to deliberate its verdict. There was nothing left for him to do but wait.

This time, however, he did not wait. With the assistance of two associate attorneys and a paralegal, he collected the exhibits, pleadings, and reams of paper and went back to his office. Hempstead had looked forward to this moment for many months. In the morning, he would leave Cincinnati and put the law behind him for a week. There was no way for Jim Hempstead to know then that the week would turn into a lifetime.

It was their second attempt to climb the Grand Teton. The price of their quest was measured only in terms of damage to relationships: it cost Jim Hempstead much more than it cost his companion, Craig Rose.

Rose was stocky and strong. He had a pale complexion and very little red hair left on top of his head. He wore a full beard that he rarely kept trimmed, and to the people who did not know them, they appeared an unlikely pair.

Landing in Salt Lake City early on a Thursday morning, they had two days and four hundred miles to travel by car before they were to meet their guides in Jackson Hole, Wyoming. In the meantime, they had no other plans and were free to do whatever they pleased.

Leaving downtown Salt Lake City, Hempstead noticed the sporadic graffiti and immigrant Mexican neighborhoods which led him to believe that Utah had changed somewhat since he had attended college there many years before. The reverse migration from California brought both the people and the culture, he thought. Nevertheless, while Utah no longer appeared completely dominated by its Mormon heritage, it seemed to him remarkably untouched by the remainder of the American civilization that surrounded it.

The barren and scrubby front of Utah's Wasatch Mountains was just as Hempstead remembered. He knew that a person had to get high up into the mountains to know them in all of their beauty.

Hempstead was driving North along Interstate 15 toward Logan, and then over the pass into Idaho and then Wyoming. Craig Rose was sitting next to him drinking a beer from the styrofoam cooler safely resting in the backseat.

"God, I haven't been to Logan since college," Hempstead told him. "Mind if we stop for a beer?"

"Just lead the way."

"There's a little bar called The Bistro that I'd like to show you," Hempstead continued. "I used to play in a band there a long time ago."

"I didn't know you played in a band. What'd you play?"

"Guitar. I thought I'd write songs that would propel me beyond some common existence," he laughed. "Back then everyone who wasn't a Mormon would come to the Bistro on the weekends. It was our lives."

"Here's to youth," Craig Rose said lifting his beer in Hempstead's direction.

They continued further along the highway before turning onto a winding two-lane road that led them down into Cache Valley where Logan sits. Hempstead drove without hesitation to a parking lot beside the old, but newly painted, structure. The weathered cedar siding to which he had been accustomed was painted bright yellow. The sign on the door did not say "The Bistro," it read instead, "The Boulevard."

When they went inside, Hempstead did not recognize a thing. The picnic tables had been replaced by sturdy fixtures with comfortable chairs and white linen tablecloths. There were colorful plastic flowers sitting in plastic vases in the center of each table.

They sat down and were immediately greeted by a happy waitress clad in a freshly starched blue apron with "The Boulevard" emblazoned on the front. She dutifully reported on the fine micro brews made in the stainless steel tanks in the cellar below them.

"God, this place has changed," Hempstead said after they had ordered. "You know, I never thought when I was playing music in here that I'd end up graduating first in my class from a law school in Ohio."

"I didn't know that you graduated first in your class."

"Why should you? A lot of good it's done for me. Graduate, get married, have a kid and then hope that he doesn't notice the absence of love between his parents."

"Hey, man. We're supposed to be having fun, remember? Don't get in one of your moods."

"See that window?" Hempstead asked pointing upward.

"Yea, what about it?"

"That's where the stage used to be. Some asshole took it down and put in that window and the light coming through it has stolen the soul of this place."

5

"We all remember things differently, Hemp."

The disappointment and disgust Hempstead was suffering was evident. "Let's get out of here," he said after it became too much.

They took to the canyon that separates northern Utah from Idaho and Wyoming. The landscape had dramatically changed from the comparative flatness and void of Ohio as they drove for a long while with no short-term agenda.

Not one thing had changed in the canyon. Sagebrush covered the lower half of the walls rising up from the road and stopping where a rocky swath cut its way across the upper part of the face. Swells of pine tree seemed to smoothly flow up and then down revealing the contours of the countless drainages that intersected with the canyon and fed the many alpine lakes strewn high along the mountains into southern Idaho.

Hempstead was thankful that the road was removing him from the threat to his memories of the old times. Time changes people, he thought, but not the mountains. For the longest while he did not say a word as he escaped to the safety of his private world and pretended that this was his life.

"I need these trips, you know, Craig?" Hempstead said when he came back.

"We both do."

"No. The mountains make me a good person, or at least the person that I think I should be. When I'm away like this, everything that should be important in my life is so obvious from the distance. But no matter how hard I try, I can't hold onto the perspective for very long once I'm back."

"You're too serious, Hemp. I think you need another beer."

They continued drinking from the bounty of cold beer stashed away in their styrofoam cooler. It was quickly becoming dusk in the mountains and the sun lowering to the West constantly changed the size, shape, and location of the shadows all about them making it appear as if they were traveling through some sort of cosmic kaleidoscope.

When they finally stopped they had been traveling for almost ten hours. They were in Afton, Wyoming --a small town situated in the pine-covered mountains surrounding Star Valley. Just as they were pulling into town, a flash of light in the distance signaled an approaching storm.

Hastily checking each of the four motels they could find on one pass down Main Street, they concluded that there were no vacancies anywhere in town. It seemed as if the entire population of Wyoming had inexplicably descended upon the little community. Putting aside an immediate notion to get back in the car and drive, they decided to enter the nearest bar in search of refreshment and perhaps some information concerning accommodations.

The Cowboy Bar was small and empty except for Jim Hempstead, Craig Rose and an older man with a couple of days white stubble about his face. He was gripping a cigarette between the tar-stained fingers of one hand and held a half-full glass of beer in the other. His ears nearly formed points at the top and he had a small pointed noise and thin lips giving him an odd elf-like appearance. Hempstead concluded that this fixture of a person was probably a perpetual patron.

Hempstead also judged that he was intruding in a place where for many generations ranchers and cowhands could feel comfortable among themselves. The old wooden bar was ornate and obviously constructed with the care and attention that was only available to people before the dawn of the television age. Years of elbows and glasses working their way against the surface of the bar had worn away just enough to make it slightly concave requiring special care in the placement of full glasses of beer. The pool table was as ornate as the bar and its battered leather-netted pockets suggested its age to be as old as the establishment. The floor was made of wood and patterned with decades of cigarette burns. Next to the old pot-bellied stove that sat in the middle of the room was a stuffed grizzly bear with large patches of hair missing. The tarnished plaque at its feet read, "Shot by Seth Davis, October 12, 1913." Hempstead could not help

7

but feel transported back in time to a location that put him at ease and in the mood for drink.

"We need to make some friends around here," Hempstead whispered and then called to the bartender. "Two beers, please."

On the wall was a hastily painted posterboard sign that said "S List." Upon it were names followed by letters that resembled some form of code. They agreed that it was a "shit list," but argued amongst themselves concerning the meaning of the remaining encrypted letters. Both were keen at taking any position in an argument, and they quickly achieved the inevitable impasse.

"What does 'B-A-G-P-I-T-A' mean?" Craig Rose finally asked the bartender.

The man did not take his eyes off of the glass that he was washing in the sink in front of him. "Being a general pain in the ass."

He pointed to the next line. "What about 'T-H-F-O,' what does that stand for?"

"Outta here 'til hell freezes over."

Craig Rose looked toward Hempstead who with a slight tilt of the head gave him some assurance that the inquiry should persist.

"And just what must one do to be the recipient of such a sanction? Is there some sort of policy manual we should review before drinking any further?"

"Nah," the bartender finally laughed and set his work aside. "Annie, the owner, is bullheaded and always right. This bar's been in her family since there was Indians around here. She runs this place pretty much as she sees fit. Fighting, mooching, or a bad check gets ya instant expulsion. For being a pain in the ass, she usually gives 'em three warnings, then they're out."

Outside the rain began to fall. Having nowhere to go, they continued to order beer and Hempstead allowed a rush of relaxation to come over him. He was no longer a lawyer, a father, a husband, or anything at all. Other than Craig Rose, nobody in the world knew where he was or what he was doing: he was free to be whatever he wanted and he savored the feeling.

Their silent friend at the end of the bar seemed deep in thought and Hempstead took it upon himself to manufacture conversation.

"I see one of those names is crossed off the list," he said. "How'd that person get back in the good graces around here?"

"He died." A question mark came about the bartender's face and he held up an empty glass.

"Sure, two more, please."

Hempstead looked around and noticed a muddy white cowboy hat hanging over the bar in an obvious place of honor. The sign below it read simply "Claude Dallas was here."

Hempstead knew that Claude Dallas had lived in the mountains and had shot a game warden who accused him of poaching. For the longest time Dallas eluded a massive FBI manhunt before finally being caught, jailed, and escaping. Hempstead had read about it in the papers and watched the drama play out on the television news. Dallas had become a modern legend of the West who Hempstead had admired for the courage to give and take a bullet. Claude Dallas was a real man, he thought, not like the digital warriors that he dealt with on a daily basis who never had to look their opposition in the eye. Hempstead was in a wild place and he liked it.

"Did Claude Dallas really drink in here?" he asked.

"Every once in a while," the bartender answered in a dead serious tone. "Until the feds caught up with him."

"Hey, what's going on?" Hempstead finally asked thinking their relationship had appropriately crossed into the familiar. "We can't find a room for miles?"

His reply was matter of fact. "It's the rodeo," he said. "Biggest damn thing to happen in these parts. Everything's full from here all the way to Jackson."

The conversation remained short, but friendly. They ordered another beer and Craig Rose put some country music on the juke box to signal them as friendly strangers.

Perhaps it was the music, but after a couple of those songs the man at the end of the bar broke his silence and called down to them in a raspy voice.

"You boys can stay at my trailer if you like." He paused momentarily to drink from his beer and wipe the remnants from his mouth. "And ya know, Colter's is havin' an all-nighter."

Had he been in Cincinnati, Hempstead would have never considered the offer, --not even heard it. But on the road and in that bar the promise meant a floor to sleep upon at a minimum, and contained the hope of an all-niter, whatever that was.

"Can you show us how to get to Colter's?" he asked.

"Just follow me." The elf guzzled the rest of his beer and slid the empty glass away. "See ya' tomorrow," he called down to the bartender.

Hempstead paid for the beer and they all left together into the rain.

Colter's had a rustic log-cabin appearance that was classic western motif. It was a large wooden complex with a hotel, restaurant, and bar all in the same building. The rooms were all taken when they walked in wet from the rain, but the lounge was relatively vacant affording them an opportunity to sit at the long oak bar.

The walls were paneled with knotty pine and shrouded with animal heads and antique brewery paraphernalia. They took seats on the stools in front of the bar and began ordering beer.

Before too long the elf abandoned them for the pool tables bothering to check back only so often as was necessary to borrow more money or con another beer. The absences were a relief to Hempstead who didn't feel like pretending friendship and the attendant responsibility for dialogue and concern. They had an on-going bet regarding

10

the elapsed time between those intervals, which Craig Rose carefully timed and recorded on a soggy paper napkin next to his beer. It was a great sport for them with the loser having to ante up to the request. During the meantime, they ordered buffalo burgers and more beer.

Hempstead was enjoying everything about where he was. He had never been in the place and yet he knew it well. He had a calculated manner that appeared to be choreographed like some dance of the bar. There was a relaxed look about him that exhibited the subtle confidence that served him so well in the courtroom. Hempstead knew when to order a beer so that it would arrive just before the one in his hands had been emptied. He knew how to look as if he were ignoring everything that was going on about him and yet observe it all at the same time. Hempstead knew how to appear to fit in and he liked the perfection. There was no misery where he was and no reason for him to go elsewhere.

"What's an all-nighter?" Craig Rose asked the woman who had been bringing them their drinks.

She let out a quick chuckle and then said, "three times a year, the state of Wyoming allows a bar to call an all-niter. The bar don't shut down for twenty-four hours." Pausing for a moment to wipe up the ring that Hempstead's glass had left upon the bar she added, "boys, if you're at all interested in a party, an all-nighter is a partier's party."

"We've got no place to stay other than the floor of a trailer. We don't even know the guy." Hempstead laughed at the thought of spending the night on some stranger's trailer floor. Shit, the elf probably didn't even remember his offer.

"You're from back East, ain't ya? I can tell by your clothes and your talk. Look," she said, "if you guys can't stay up the night with the rest of us, I'll get ya a place upstairs."

It was getting dark outside and the place began to fill as the seats that they had occupied earlier at the empty bar became prime real estate. Tired from a long day of traveling, Hempstead was relieved to have a place to stay and curious in some anthropological sense to explore an all-niter.

"I wonder who the person was who thought up the idea of an all-nighter?" Hempstead asked when she was gone. "I mean, how did that concept ever show up as an agenda in the legislature? I'd like to have heard the debate over whether an all-nighter is a good thing or not."

By that time Craig Rose's ears had turned deep purple from the drink. It was a hideous and telling affliction the sight of which disturbed Hempstead like minor infirmities tend to do with people who spend time together.

"I don't know," he said, "but I think it's an inspired idea that was probably long over due. My guess is there wasn't much of a debate."

They both laughed and raised their glasses in a salute to the Wyoming legislature. For a long while afterwards there wasn't any talk between them. They listened to the music and Hempstead forgave his friend's crimson ears.

Craig Rose finally broke that silence as the hours upon hours of alcohol consumption finally took him over.

"You know," he said, "I've always played by the rules. If the speed limit says '65,' then that's what I drive."

"So, what's your point?" Hempstead was enjoying his anonymous freedom and was not in the mood for another philosophical conversation. At least not one that he hadn't started.

It was true that Craig Rose lived his life by the rules and that had always annoyed him. It was also true that their conversations rarely ventured below an innocuous surface that they both understood and accepted. They had perfected a safe and comfortable banter between them that revolved around stating the obvious and leaving little room for disagreement. Hempstead did not think that it was time to deviate from their routine.

"I live by the rules, and that's what I need," he continued. "I'm happy that way. You ... " He didn't finish his thought and didn't need to.

"What are you talking about?" Hempstead could feel the anger begin to warm his body.

"You have the curse."

12

"What the fuck are you talking about?" He snapped again before thinking better of having opened the door for Craig Rose to ramble on.

"Come on, man, the curse of options," he said. "Most people come into this life and struggle to find what they were called upon to do. When they eventually do, they live out their lives with some sense of purpose. You can do anything you want. You will never find your purpose because your purpose can be anything you want it to be."

The band was loudly playing country music and a sea of cowboy hats began to ebb and sway to a two-step beat around the dance floor. Certainly there were more people in Colter's for the all-nighter than lived in all of Afton. There was more silence between them and Hempstead was momentarily relieved that his stool mate had apparently become distracted from the conversation.

But Craig Rose was relentless. "Think about it," he said. "Every night cave men must have come back to their caves and just been happy as shit not to have been killed and eaten that day. They could find purpose in having survived through the day. We haven't suffered shit. No depression, no war, no fucking plague." He paused, drew up his mouth and shook his head as if to punctuate the supposedly sublime nature of his observations. "Our generation must create and survive its own pain."

"With all the fucking misery created by all my apparent options, you'd think I'd be happy as hell." Hempstead didn't bother to ask Craig Rose what petty turbulence he had overcome to make him so contented.

Instead, he became distracted by a group of drunk and rowdy women standing to his right. One womans' elbow hit him in the face as she turned to deliver four tiny glasses of dark-colored liquid to her friends.

"This stuff is 'fuck you up bad.'" Elaine Lois Sutter did not otherwise offer to excuse herself.

She appeared to be somewhere between twenty and thirty years old and intoxicated. Her brown hair hung down to the sweatshirt covering her shoulders and she wore tan suede

13

cowboy boots that emerged from beneath her faded jeans. Hempstead was pleasantly struck by her beauty and by the end of the painful conversation he had been having with Craig Rose.

"Jaegermeister!" the women shouted together.

"Fuck you up bad," added Elaine.

Elaine Sutter was born and raised in Santa Monica, California until she was eleven years old. She moved to Afton to live with her mother's brother when her parents divorced. Her earliest memories did not include the incest and "special time" that her father had inflicted upon her from the time she was eight until she reached puberty: those memories did not surface until she was twenty and were never shared with anyone.

Elaine's earliest recollection was of a father who would tinker and concoct. She recalls the axle parts and other automotive components that lined the way from her bedroom to the bathroom. She knew their precise location so that at night she could automatically pick up her feet and avoid the consequences of a nocturnal confrontation with them while maintaining her dream-like state.

She remembers being in a car when her father was pulled over by the police and the resulting nightmare when the officers--many of whom were radioed in for the occasion-- attempted to determine the make of the automobile. Although it seems the title listed the car as a Mercury, Elaine's father had cut two cars in half and married a Ford with a Mercury--her family called it "the Forcury." Elaine would always suppose that the purpose of that undertaking was to provoke just such an official quandary.

William Grey was Elaine Sutter's uncle, who she still called "Uncle Billy." He had learned mountaineering techniques in the army during World War II and apart from the scar where the bullet had entered his stomach, the only thing he brought home from the war were knowledge and training. On the weekends he would take Elaine up into the mountains where he taught her how to handle a rope and climb shear rock faces. When they weren't in the mountains they would often sit around the house and endlessly race each other to the conclusion of a perfect knot. No matter what they were doing, Elaine and Uncle Billy talked to one another about everything except her father. He had told her many times during those talks about how he had chosen to let the bullet give him life and so he wore it as a reminder on a chain around his neck.

Through it all Elaine had come to be independent and to know the outdoors. Her escape from the incest and insanity was outside. She became a ski instructor at Snowbird, Utah. She also became a sometimes mountain guide--an experienced mountaineer respected and trusted by other climbers. Before she moved out of his home, Uncle Billy had given her his bullet. Several years before she had a little bit of it melted down and formed into the crude shape of a mountain and she wore it attached to a thin leather band around her wrist.

Jim Hempstead tapped her on the shoulder to get her attention. "Tell me about this Jaegermeister ritual."

"It's fuck you up bad," she said and turned indifferently back to her friends.

"So, I hear."

She swung around again, squinted her eyes at him, and then redirected her gaze to her friends who were now dancing together.

"You're not from around here are you?" She still did not take her eyes off the participants on the dance floor. "These cowboys can't stay in the saddle very long."

Thus began a game that Hempstead enjoyed and Craig Rose liked to watch. Hempstead was miserable but he was faithful. He would never play the courting game a moment longer than it took to revitalize his ego.

This game began when Elaine Sutter grabbed his hand and jerked him to the dance floor. "Let's go!" she shouted.

Hempstead didn't know how to dance to the music, but it didn't matter because she took control. They danced palm-to-palm, face-to-face, and very slowly even though the beat was very quick. Hempstead felt the warmth of excitement come to him. He had always believed that you could tell how a person made love by the way that they danced. Elaine's manner was slow, passionate, deliberate, and right in time.

"Look around," she said. "You're not making any friends in here." She smiled and looked directly into his eyes.

Hempstead knew she was right. The locals were congregating and protectively staring down the intruder from the east who was dancing with one of their women. He didn't care, though--he was more concerned about her eyes. She had beautiful teal-green eyes unlike any he had ever seen before. He could feel Elaine pouring herself into his being through those eyes.

"Let's get a drink," he offered before another song could start.

She took him immediately by the hand and led him to the bar where she ordered their drinks.

"Jaegermiester, fuck you up bad!" Elaine slammed her empty shot glass on the bar.

Now, Hempstead was really excited, but not about the Jaegermiester, which he believed was too sweet and heavy to be a real drink. Her attitude coupled with her beauty was the potent mix that was intoxicating him.

"So, what do you do?" She was almost yelling to be heard over the music.

"I'm a fucking lawyer," he yelled back.

"Why do you say it that way?"

"It's a long story, but trust me, there's nothing special about being a lawyer."

"Never thought there was."

They continued to dance and drink for a long while. Jim Hempstead had long ago forgotten about Craig Rose and how tired he was. He was in a completely different time and place than he had eaten when he left Ohio over fourteen hours earlier.

Between dances they sat next to each other on wooden stools at a small elevated table away from the bar where they could feel the warmth from the fireplace. Hempstead rested his forearms on the flat surface and held his beer with both hands slowly tilting it back and forth. She was sitting with her thigh touching his knee. When Elaine reached for her beer, she allowed her pinkie to brush up against his hand. Hempstead did not move. He understood the message but did not know from moment to moment how he would ultimately respond. Hempstead didn't have to wait long.

"Look," she said, "I know you're married." Elaine paused for a moment and looked around before whispering in his ear. "So, how's it feel?"

"How does what feel?"

"I love your shirt." Her hands were now pressed firmly against his chest. "I want to see it lying on the floor at the foot of my bed in the morning."

"I've got a son."

"So, how does it feel?" She asked again mockingly louder than before.

"How does what feel?"

"You're married, you have a son, and in fifteen minutes you'll be fucking my brains out."

"I can't." Hempstead forced the words from his mouth. He had been here before, but never had those words been so difficult.

"You're not too old are you?" She taunted. "You will never see me again. You don't have to worry."

"I'm not, but I never have … " he didn't finish.

"You need another fuck you up bad," she said. "Stay right there, I'll go get 'em."

After she disappeared into the crowd, Hempstead escaped to the safety of his room feeling certain that Elaine Lois Sutter could handle the drinks and herself for the rest of the evening.

When they awoke in the morning, the hall outside their room was littered with cowboys who spent the night where they dropped. There was no sign of Elaine who had vanished into the vapor of an all-nighter.

Leaving for Jackson Hole before the repairs had even begun on the shattered windows and broken doors, they heard someone in the lobby say that it was not as bad as it had been the past couple of years.

They were on the road and the sun had not yet crested the mountains to the east when Hempstead reached for a beer.

Craig Rose, who was driving, looked over toward him and said, "a Red Stripe, huh? That's a great morning beer. Didn't you get enough last night?"

"I didn't know we were married."

"Apparently neither did your green-eyed friend. So'd you guys go for a ride up the canyon?"

"You know better than that."

"Think we'll start callin' you 'Catch n' Release.' Mr. Catch n' Release Hempstead. Always lettin' everything go."

"At least I can still catch a fish. By the way, what time did you leave last night?"

"Oh, now you're concerned about me. Let's just say I didn't want to spook away your fish."

They were rapidly approaching Targhee National Forest and the Snake River Canyon. It was all as fantastic as he had remembered. The steep mountain slopes were covered with pine trees and cottonwoods. The canyon walls dropped to where the Snake River slithered far below. But as the road wound and climbed high through the beauty, Hempstead could not take his mind off the practice of law he had left thousands of miles behind.

He struggled to put down the contempt and self-pity that was welling up inside of him. When he hated something, he hated everything, and hated it all good and hard. He didn't need those feelings here--this is where he wanted to be, and he couldn't afford to have this place taken from him, too.

It made him wonder why he ever went back to Ohio. Indeed, part of his anguish arose from the consequences of the misguided, and ultimately binding, priorities of youth. He had wanted the money, the prestige, and the professional stature of a lawyer. He quickly learned, however, that being a lawyer did not guarantee money, did not necessarily bring prestige, and did not at all involve a profession. The law had revealed itself to him as a ruthless business where the enemy was as much his own partners as it was opposing counsel.

He discovered that value in a law firm was not measured by talent, but instead by the hour and by the client. The internal firm politics resulting from the posturing for hours, clients, and money, resembled to him a dysfunctional family at a holiday party. It was not surprising to him that the pressures of the business had cast many a respectable and intelligent human into the throws of depression, drinking, and extra-marital affairs. He had managed to avoid only the latter. For now, these adventures provided the excitement he needed in his life.

As they continued to make their way over Teton Pass, they had "Little Feat" blaring on the tape deck. They never left for these trips without their music and it slowly began to take Jim Hempstead's mind off of his misery.

"Little Feat died with Lowell George," Craig Rose said to no one in particular and while grabbing for his first beer of the day.

That was a point over which there was no debate between them, and a point that was made whenever they played "Little Feat," which was often.

"That's for damn sure," Hempstead said, "we're fucking older than Lowell was when he died and we haven't done shit."

"What's the best rock n' roll song of all time, Hemp?" Craig Rose asked rhetorically.

"No brainer. 'Cinnamon Girl.'" Hempstead reached over and slapped the awaiting hand.

"Well put it on, man!"

Hempstead hunted for the tape from among those that were cast about the car and eventually found it in the mess of empty cans and bottles surrounding his feet. They did not talk any further once the melodic tune began.

After a while, Hempstead reached into his back pocket and pulled out a hastily folded brochure that he had been sitting on all day. It was a pamphlet that he had taken from a

19

counter at Colter's the evening before. With nothing else to do, he read the tale reprinted inside:

ACCOUNTS OF JOHN COLTER'S ESCAPE FROM THE BLACKFEET[1]

This man came to St. Louis in May, 1810, in a small canoe, from the headwaters of the Missouri, a distance of three thousand miles, which he traversed in thirty days. I saw him on his arrival, and received from him an account of his adventures after he had separated from Lewis and Clark's party at the headwaters of the Missouri, Colter, observing an appearance of abundance of beaver there, got permission to remain and hunt for some time, which he did in company with a man by the name of Dixon, who had traversed the immense tract of country from St. Louis to the headwaters of the Missouri alone.

Soon after he separated from Dixon, and in company with a hunter named Potts; and aware of the hostility of the Blackfeet Indians, one of whom had been killed by Lewis, they set their traps at night, and took them up early in the morning, remaining concealed during the day. They were examining their traps early one morning, in a creek about six miles from that branch of the Missouri called Jefferson Fork, and were ascending in a canoe, when they suddenly heard a great noise, resembling the trampling of animals; but they could not ascertain the fact, as the high, perpendicular banks on each side of the river impeded their view. Colter immediately pronounced it to be occasioned by Indians, and advised an instant retreat; but was accused of cowardice by Potts, who insisted that the noise was caused by buffaloes, and they proceeded on. In a few minutes afterwards their doubts were removed by a party of Indians making their appearance on both sides of the creek, to the amount of five or six hundred, who beckoned them to come ashore. As retreat was now impossible, Colter turned the head of the

---

[1] "Accounts of John Colter's Escape from the Blackfeet," from Bradbury, John. *Travels in the Interior America.* London: Sherwood, Neely, and Jones. (1819), reprinted in Chittendon, H.M. *The American Fur Trade of the Far West.*

canoe to the shore; and at the moment of its touching, an Indian seized the rifle belonging to Potts; but Colter, who is a remarkably strong man, immediately retook it, and handed it to Potts, who remained in the canoe, and on receiving it pushed off into the river. He had scarcely quitted the shore when an arrow was shot at him, and he cried out, "Colter, I am wounded." Colter remonstrated with him on the folly of attempting to escape, and urged him to come ashore. Instead of complying, he instantly leveled his rifle at an Indian, and shot him dead on the spot. This conduct, situated as he was, may appear to have been an act of madness; but it was doubtless the effect of sudden and sound reasoning; for if taken alive, he must have expected to be tortured to death, according to custom. He was instantly pierced with arrows so numerous that, to use the language of Colter, "he was made a riddle of."

They now seized Colter, stripped him entirely naked, and began to consult on the manner in which he should be put to death. They were first inclined to set him up as a mark to shoot at; but the chief interfered, and seizing him by the shoulder, asked him if he could run fast. Colter, who had been some time amongst the kee-kat-sa, or Crow Indians, had in a considerable degree acquired the Blackfoot language, and was also well acquainted with Indian customs. He knew that he had now to run for his life, with the dreadful odds of five or six hundred against him, and those armed Indians; therefore he cunnibly replied that he was a very bad runner, although he was considered by the hunters as remarkably swift. The chief now commanded the party to remain stationary, and led Colter out on the prairie three or four hundred yards, and released him, bidding him to save himself if he could. At that instant the horrid war whoop sounded in the ears of poor Colter, who, urged with the hope of preserving his life, ran with a speed at which he was himself surprised. He proceeded towards the Jefferson Fork, having to traverse a plain six miles in breadth, abounding with prickly pear, on which he was every instant treading with his naked feet. He ran nearly halfway across

21

the plain before he ventured to look over his shoulder, when he perceived that the Indians were very much scattered, and that he had gained ground to a considerable distance from the main body; but one Indian, who carried a spear, was much before all the rest, and not more than a hundred yards from him. A faint gleam of hope now cheered the heart of Colter; he derived confidence from the belief that escape was within the bounds of possibility; but that confidence was nearly fatal to him, for he exerted himself to such a degree that the blood gushed from his nostrils, and soon almost covered the forepart of his body.

He had now arrived within a mile of the river, when he distinctly heard the appalling sound of footsteps behind him, and every instant expected to feel the spear of his pursuer. Again he turned his head, and saw the savage not twenty yards in front of him. Determined if possible to avoid the expected blow, he suddenly stopped, turned round, and spread out his arms. The Indian, surprised by the suddenness of the action and perhaps of the bloody appearance of Colter, also attempted to stop; but exhausted with running, he fell whilst endeavoring to throw his spear, which stuck in the ground and broke in his hand. Colter instantly snatched up the pointed part, with which he pinned him to the earth, and then continued his flight. The foremost of the Indians, on arriving at the place, stopped till others came up to join them, when they set up a hideous yell. Every moment of this time was improved by Colter, who, although fainting and exhausted, succeeded in gaining the skirting of the cottonwood trees, on the borders of the fork, through which he ran and plunged into the river. Fortunately for him, a little below this place there was an island, against the upper point of which a raft of drift timber, had lodged. He dived under the raft, and after several efforts, got his head above the water amongst the trunks of trees, covered over with smaller wood to the depth of several feet. Scarcely had he secured himself when the Indians arrived on the river, screeching and yelling, as Colter expressed it, "like so many devils." They were frequently on the raft during the day, and *were seen through the chinks by Colter, who was congratulating himself on his escape, until the idea arose that they might set the raft on fire.*

In horrible suspense he remained until night, when hearing no more of the Indians, he dived under the raft, and swam silently down the river to a considerable distance, when he landed and traveled all night. Although happy in having escaped from the Indians, his situation was still dreadful; he was completely naked, under a burning sun; the soles of his feet were entirely filled with the thorns of the prickly pear; he was hungry, and had no means of killing game, although he saw abundance around him, and was at least seven days journey from Lisa's Fort, on the Bighorn branch of the Roche Jaune River. These were circumstances under which almost any man but an American hunter would have despaired. He arrived at the fort in seven days, having subsisted on a root much esteemed by the Indians of the Missouri, now known by naturalists as psoralea esculenta.

"Now that guy had to be one fulfilled mother fucker." He crumpled up the paper and cast it into the back of the car.

"What?"

"Nothing."

The pass soon gave way to the vast expanse of Jackson Hole. As they continued their approach to Grand Teton National Park, the jagged peaks of the Teton mountain range suddenly came into view.

"The Tetons are fucking mountains," announced Craig Rose. "I mean, no foothills, no warning, you look up, and there they are ... sheer fucking rock going straight up."

Hempstead snickered to himself. "Just imagine how lonely those fur traders must have been to see these mountains and name them after giant tits."

"You see," Craig Rose said, "even back then women were able to wield their influence over men from thousands of miles away. One way or another, they're always trying to ruin their boy's trips."

They both laughed and enjoyed their united sense of understanding.

The cloudless sky was deep blue and broken only by the granite peak that is the Grand Teton with the massive ridge created by its imposing counterparts stretching northward as far as they could see. The object of their journey towered before them and looked impossible to climb from their vantage far below.

It was then that Hempstead began thinking about the otter. There is a snow field directly below the summit and if the snow during the winter was excessive, it takes on the shape of an inverted otter. If the otter was there, then the chances were that there was still much snow up high making an ascent of the mountain face unlikely, or very difficult and unpredictable at best.

Hempstead had learned about the otter during their failed attempt to climb the Grand Teton several years before. He had learned many lessons about the mountains that year. He had learned just how cold it can be at 12,000 feet in the middle of August. He had learned that, even with guides, in the mountains he was responsible for his own well-being. He had grown to expect the worst and enjoy it.

It was difficult for Craig Rose to drive and make out the details of the mountain at the same time, although he tried and on several occasions the diversion had sent them directly into the path of on-coming traffic.

"Do you see the otter?" he finally asked with some measure of surrender in his voice.

Hempstead took a few moments to carefully examine the situation. "Nope," he said. "No otter this year!"

The joint jubilation they felt following the otter-free proclamation lead them to simultaneously break out in unison, "no otter, no otter, no otter," mimicking the "no rain" chant from Woodstock.

Jim Hempstead was able at the same time to reach into the cooler for another beer. Things were finally beginning to look very good.

By the time they reached the Climbers' Ranch, it wasn't even noon. The ranch is situated at the base of the Grand Teton offering a picturesque view of the Teton Range. For five dollars a night, payable on a voluntary basis, climbers could stay in primitive cabins.

Like any great society, law had evolved at the ranch that was designed to ensure its continued existence. Over it's twenty-year history, two important rules had emerged --and they were the only rules that there were. First, there could be no fires in the cabins. Second, all food had to be stored high in a tree so as not to attract the bears. They were rules that even the most renegade climbers agreed with, or at least generally abided by.

The cabin was empty when they arrived, save for six plywood bunk beds and a single toilet. They threw out their sleeping bags to stake their territory and then headed into town.

After downing several cold beers in the darkness of the Silver Dollar Bar, they left, walking past its souvenir shop and into the arid warmth of the sun on Cache Street. Thirty yards down the wooden-planked sidewalk they rounded into an alley and climbed the stairs fixed to the exterior of the Rancher Bar. Outside on the verandah they took seats at a round white metal table under the protection of a Cinzano umbrella. From their vantage they could watch a crowd of people taking pictures of one another in front of the large arch made of dried antlers that marked the entrance into Town Square which was directly across the street from them.

They spent most of the day wandering around in and out of those bars and Jim Hempstead tried unsuccessfully to purge the notion that what was left of the "old west" was vanishing before his eyes. He told Craig Rose that "twenty years ago you couldn't give your life to find a twenty dollar bottle of wine in this town." The Jackson that Hempstead had known many years before was a working town that just happened to be in the most beautiful place on earth.

All of Jackson's promotional literature encouraged that cowboy image but with the infusion of west coast celebrities and Madison Avenue boutiques it had lost the battle. Or maybe, Hempstead thought, it had won. He couldn't understand why these people had chosen to do this to themselves.

The air occasionally filled with sickening exhaust fumes wafting up from the tour buses on the street below and before too much longer, Hempstead was gone. He hated the sight of all the people--he hated them for taking something from him. They had turned Jackson from the rugged into the quaint and he hated each one of them good and hard for it.

Craig Rose eventually lost their bet concerning the number of tourists that they could count having their pictures taken in front of the antler arch. But the mockery didn't work. When he had endured all he could, Hempstead demanded the usual and readily available escape from his suffering--they had to get in the car and drive. They followed Flat Creek out of town for destinations unknown-- maybe they would drive into Teton Village or maybe they would follow Teton Pass back into some small town in rural Idaho.

Midnight eventually found them drunk in the little town of Wilson, which was just ten miles outside of Jackson but thirty years away. They knew at the Stagecoach they could avoid the platinum-carded outsiders who had taken over the drinking establishments in Jackson.

Except for the neon beer lights strung up against its outer wooden wall, the structure looked more like a motel than a bar. But its gravel parking lot was overloaded with pickup trucks and the Stagecoach was not a motel.

When they walked inside the locals were square dancing all around them as they tried to edge their way to the bar. Their beer had just been delivered when, without missing a note, the fiddler suddenly jumped up on the bar and juked his way down the entire length without regard to the bottles, cans, ashtrays, or arms along the way. He jumped down at the other end and mingled his way into a perfectly timed do-si-do. The crowd was frenzied by his antics. They were shouting, singing and stomping their feet to the music.

In the midst of the delirium, Jim Hempstead became absorbed again in his drunken thoughts.

"Do you suppose there are others like us, Craig?" he asked. "Middle-aged fucks who are bored as shit and have done nothing with their lives." He was immediately pissed off that this time he had started such a conversation and wanted to take the question back. It was too late.

Craig Rose laughed. "Are you suggesting that you are the first person to endure a mid-life crisis?"

"No." It was especially disturbing that Craig Rose had suggested his misery was a universal one. If Hempstead had to suffer, he wanted the pain to belong only to him. "It keeps following me, Craig."

"What keeps following you, Hemp?" He asked not at all listening for an answer.

"My nemesis. It's followed me from one lifetime to another always seeking to ruin me. I never know how or when it will manifest itself or how it will suck the life from me. I just know that it has in the past and it's doing it again. I've got to kill it. If I could just kill it then everything would be okay--it would be all right forever. I just don't know how."

"Oh man, that's right. It's your birthday. Happy birthday! I'm sorry, I forgot … ."

Hempstead swept his empty beer can aside putting an end to whatever it was that Craig Rose was about to say. "Fuck my birthday," he said.

"I think I need to buy you a birthday beer. That's what I think."

Ignoring him, Hempstead stood and walked to the door. "I'm dead," he said. "I'm the living dead."

As they drove, the full moon hung over the mountains lighting up all there was to see and Jim Hempstead became lost in the dreamy backdrop of the extraordinary landscape. When they returned to the ranch they were cautious not to disturb the others who had arrived and fallen asleep in their absence. Lying down in his bunk to the silence of a Wyoming night, Hempstead surrendered to dreams he would never remember.

27

Chapter 2

Early the next morning before any tourists were up, Jim Hempstead and Craig Rose enjoyed a large breakfast at a local diner under the suspicious gaze of the weathered ranchers that sat all about them. Indulging themselves with enormous amounts of bacon, eggs, toast, and coffee, they reasoned that it would be their last good meal for two days and that they would need the energy.

When they had finished, they drove the short distance back into Teton National Park to check in with their guides. Leaving the car parked in the Jenny Lake visitor center parking area, they walked across a little wooden-planked foot bridge that crossed over a clear-running stream. From there, a dirt path lead them toward a small deep brown wooden building that had an assortment of backpacks leaning up against it. Walking inside and up to the counter, Hempstead gave their names to the woman standing behind it.

"Hey, Princessa, your clients are here," she called to the people in the room behind her.

Jim Hempstead and Craig Rose were studying the pictures of climbing success that were proudly displayed on the walls of the guide house and paid no attention to the woman as she silently came up and stood behind them. She was studying index cards with information about her clients written on them.

"Hi, my name is Elaine," she said when she had finished.

They turned and instantly recognized her.

"Shit," Hempstead thought, "I never asked her what she did."

Perhaps it was the smoke-laden light that night. Maybe he had forgotten it through the haze of alcohol and

28

exhaustion. But there in that light of day, she had remarkable natural beauty. She wore no make up, and didn't need to. Her green eyes and tanned skin exuded health. She had her sandy-brown hair pulled back in a small ponytail save for a wispy strand that dangled down over her right eye. She appeared taller than he recalled and was wearing a T-shirt and baggy shorts exposing her lean and muscular limbs. Except for a worn leather bracelet tied in a square knot around her ankle, she wore no jewelry.

"Well, you weren't lying, were you," she said. "You guys really are lawyers."

Hempstead was at a loss for words, realizing how the tables had turned. If at Colter's he thought he had some measure of control, it was now certainly all hers.

She continued studying the client cards. "I see you guys want a shot at the Grand again."

Hempstead took her statement as if she somehow thought less of him because of his failed attempt before. Now he wondered what else was on the card.

Hempstead knew that guides make notes about their clients on those cards so that if they ever come back their new guides will have better insight into their climbing abilities and personalities. So he wondered what Elaine was learning from his card. Did it say how he refused to get out of his sleeping bag with the rest of the climbers because he was too cold? Perhaps it told her how his leg would shake uncontrollably when he was scared and on a steep pitch. His guide at the time had referred to it as "sewing-machine leg."

Whatever the information, Elaine gave no clues. With each shuffle of a card she was quietly tearing him apart. Neither did she say anything about his sudden departure from Colter's, which made it even worse. He was about to place his life in the hands of a woman whom he had abandoned without explanation just two nights before.

"We're gonna do it this year," Craig Rose said, apparently still oblivious to the moment.

"Okay, we'll see," she said. "That is, if you're not too old." Her smirk was directed at Hempstead. "Let's go see what you can do."

She picked up her day pack and headed for the large wooden boat that would carry them across Jenny Lake to the practice cliffs where she would judge their abilities for herself. The water gurgled from the idling motor as the captain waited for them to come aboard. At the dock the clean mountain air became tainted by the smoky billows of the burning oil and gas mixture spewing from the engine.

But the pungent petroleum scent quickly disappeared and the smooth ride out onto the lake offered a fantastic view of the Alp-like mountains rising up before them. The water was clear so that they could easily see the trout swimming twenty feet below, just above the pebbled bottom.

Elaine handed Hempstead a climbing rope and asked him to practice coiling it. He felt relieved to be pretending to work with the rope. It provided a momentary explanation for his inability to make conversation. His reprieve was short-lived, however, as they were shortly docking on the other side of the lake.

From the boat they hiked virtually straight up the steep mountain slope. Hempstead's legs were pounding and he was breathing hard from the effort and altitude. She led them to a nearly vertical rock wall about one hundred and fifty feet high and a three hundred yard vertical scramble through boulders off the trail.

When she stopped she handed them one end of the rope and told them to practice tying themselves into it with an overhand bowline knot. In the meantime she began measuring the rest of the rope into three equal segments tying loops into it along the way to secure into their harnesses.

While she wasn't looking at them, Craig Rose held out his rope so that Hempstead could tie the knot for him --Rose never had learned how to tie a good knot and it often proved particularly embarrassing when their guides discovered the fact for the first time high up on a mountain. As he had done so often in the past, Hempstead hastily tied the knot quietly while sternly insisting that Craig Rose needed to learn how to tie his own knots. It was far too early into the venture for the information on the cards to be confirmed.

Elaine came back to them when she was done with the rope. "Do you guys remember how to belay?" she asked. "You know, in the mountains trust in your companions is more important than money on Wall Street."

Hempstead felt certain that her reference to trust had as much to do with him leaving her at Colter's as it did with safety concerns. If she kept punishing him like this, it was going to be a very long three days.

"We've done a lot of belaying," Craig Rose answered, "but it's good we have a chance to practice again down here before we go up high." He proudly held his knot up high for her to see.

"All right, then, a little refresher." She wrapped the rope around her waist to demonstrate. "When you belay a climber, make sure that your body is fixed and secure. As the climber comes toward you pull the rope keeping it tight between the two of you. Remember, never take your brake hand off the rope. If someone falls, you'll be able to hold. Got it?"

With Elaine in the lead, they climbed a series of moderately steep pitches concentrating on enhancing their rope handling abilities. Below them on the trail a crowd of on-lookers had gathered to study their progress. It did not take long for Craig Rose and Jim Hempstead to refresh their climbing skills and Elaine was silently relieved that, unlike many of her clients, they appeared able on the rock.

At noon they sat on top of a ledge looking down upon Jenny Lake. For lunch Elaine carved them large chunks of salami and cheese and dashed them with Tabasco. After eating they practiced rappelling down a one hundred foot incline in preparation for their escape from the summit of the Grand Teton. Hempstead enjoyed the free-fall like feeling that came with the controlled descent down the rope and he wished they could do it several more times.

31

It was nearly four o'clock when they were finished. They watched as Elaine sorted through and counted her collection of the varied-shaped protection devices she had placed and removed in the rock countless times throughout the day making sure that she had left nothing behind.

"You guys check out all right. We can give the Complete Ridge a go if you like."

She went on to tell them how most ascents of the Grand Teton are made by the Upper Exum Ridge. The route was named for Glenn Exum, the first person to climb it. It is not a particularly difficult climb, but it offers sufficient exposure to give the average climber their money's worth.

Hempstead knew all that: it was the route that he and Craig Rose had failed to climb due to weather on their first attempt. Elaine went on to explain that the complete Exum Ridge is a much more technical and difficult climb. Hempstead knew that too so at first he took it as a compliment that she would offer them the opportunity. A short moment later he thought that maybe she was simply setting him up to fail again. It was the heavy price that she would extract for his abandonment.

Craig Rose squinted his eyes and twisted his head sideways staring down Hempstead as he spoke. "I don't know," he said. "I want to summit and the best shot is the upper ridge."

"Do you want a summit or a challenge?" she asked.

They were looking at each other and it was apparent to Elaine that they needed to privately caucus before a decision was made.

"Look," she said, "you don't have to make up your minds until base camp. You two talk it over and let me know. We'll meet at seven tomorrow morning. Any questions?"

"Why do they call you Princessa?" Hempstead asked.

She smiled, turned her back, and began walking down to the boat.

"Seven o'clock gentlemen," she called back to them. "I'd tell you to get a good night's sleep, but I already know

32

you guys like to go to bed early." She paused for a moment and then turned back to them. "And you better practice your knots tonight."

They were at the trailhead early. It was a cool morning and the sky was clear. Barely fifty yards away from them stood a bull moose slurping up vegetation from the swampy marsh spilling out from the stream. Jim Hempstead and Craig Rose were virtually oblivious to their mammal cousin as they nervously worked securing their packs while waiting for Elaine to arrive.

The sound of a weak sputtering engine broke the morning silence and grew louder as the once white and rusted-out Volkswagen bus launched the dust from the gravel road high up into the air in the wake behind it. When it came to a stop beside them Elaine jumped out of the passenger side and walked toward them.

"Guys, I'd like for you to meet Dave Lohr," she said without hesitation. "We call him 'The Shaman.'"

They exchanged pleasantries while Hempstead was wondering just who the stranger was and why climbers felt so compelled to give each other nicknames.

"Dave has been guiding with us for fifteen years and just returned from Patagonia where he put up an awesome route on Cerro Tore. He will be guiding with me on this climb," she told them as she put her hand on his shoulder. "Some people call him 'The Shaman' because of his mysterious ability to become one with the rock and pull off miracle climbs, but I think there's more to it than that."

Elaine had answered his question.

Dave Lohr was slender, in good shape and did not at all look to be his fifty-six years. He had a crew cut that barely divulged the sandy-blond hair that outlined his sun-darkened face. Lohr had been climbing since the early days in Yosemite and, by choice, was one of the few left from those days who had not made millions by starting his own outdoor clothing company.

"Elaine tells me we might be doing the Complete Ridge," he said.

"We really haven't decided." Craig Rose again appeared disappointed that the issue of the Complete Ridge had resurfaced.

Lohr glanced over toward Elaine and rolled his eyes. "Well, we'll have some time to talk about it on the hike up."

They were already teaming up against him and Hempstead stood silent in quiet humiliation.

"Have you boys had enough water so that you're pissing clear?" she asked. "It's a long day and you gotta stay hydrated. There won't be a good place to get water until we reach the meadows."

Hempstead could not bear to talk publicly about bodily functions --especially in front of a woman. She was pouring it on so he did not directly answer her but acknowledged he was ready to begin by picking up his pack and putting it on his back.

The trail began in the cool shade of the pine forest that sits at the base of the mountain. It was still wet from the dew as they followed a stream that has its origin in the glaciers and snow fields high above. For a long while it was a reasonably flat hike and the smell of pine trees abounded. After several hours they came upon open fields of brilliant and multi-colored wild flowers where they began to gain altitude with the many switch-backs that zig-zagged them up to a canyon. They were conserving their energy so the pace was slow and measured. But as the route became steep and direct and Hempstead's thighs began to burn with pain. He could feel the straps from his pack digging into his shoulders from the weight of the load, which already felt much heavier than when he had begun only two hours earlier.

Even so, Hempstead was not interested in the mountains around him or his discomfort. He remained lost in Elaine's beauty and the stealthy punishment she was inflicting upon him. He watched her move and breathe as she hiked. He became obsessed with her legs. He watched as one leg accepted her weight causing her muscles to flex into a rock hard sculpture and then relax as her stride shifted her weight to the other leg and the process repeated itself over and over again.

With each step his mind became more and more tortured with thoughts of the men that must have been with her. He was certain that there were many crushed egos lying in her wake. Before too long he would simply be another of them.

When they finally reached the canyon, the path became flat again but was made difficult by boulders the size of automobiles that covered the trail. They jumped from rock to rock careful to keep the weight of their packs from shifting and throwing them off-balance. After they were through the boulder field, they stopped as the day became warmer to remove some clothing. Elaine had on only a white sports bra and shorts and Hempstead was more certain than ever that she was the most attractive person he had ever met.

As they rested, they snacked on chocolate and drank much of the water they had brought with them. But Jim Hempstead was less interested in eating than he was in coming up with just the right words to recapture Elaine's attention which had apparently been left at Colter's. He remained at a loss for anything to say that he felt was not contrived so he sat silent and tormented.

After about fifteen minutes, they put on their packs and continued on up to the meadows. Hempstead turned around after some more time and noticed the lakes in the valley that were growing distant below. Far ahead and much higher was a glacier that would lead them to the saddle between the mountains where they would spend the night.

The sun was hot when they finally arrived at the meadows. They were situated far below a cirque of impressive and cathedral-like rocky peaks. There were streams running all around them and further up the trail a large waterfall cascaded down from high above the timberline. The landscape about them was a lush green color and peppered with fluorescent tents occupied by people without the desire or ambition to go higher.

Elaine dropped her pack. "We'll eat lunch here," she said.

It was warm and the men removed their shirts and laid upon the rock slabs that lead down to the stream. Craig Rose busied himself while coaxing a marmot closer to him with scraps of food while Dave Lohr walked down to the stream to fill his water bottle.

He called out to them. "Come and get it guys, this is last chance for a while."

They went down and joined him to replenish their water bottles, and once back on the rock, they ate cheese and crackers while Hempstead admired the view and Craig Rose turned his attention back to the recalcitrant marmot.

After a few more minutes, Elaine got up and climbed over the boulder ridge and started walking out of sight of the men. "I've got to go check out the scenery."

The moment she was gone, Hempstead asked Lohr why she was called "Princessa."

"Can't you tell? She is the princess of the mountains," the Shaman said swirling his arms and gesturing at the landscape.

"Yea, right," Hempstead said eager to hear the story before Elaine came back.

"Okay, all right. She was climbing Chimborazo down in Ecuador. When bad weather hit, she was stranded in a hut with a group of Austrian and Italian climbers. Seems each of the gentlemen climbers made a run at her. I guess it was some sort of an assembly line effort." Dave Lohr was smiling and shaking his head. "People who saw it say it was a sight to see. Elaine just sat their and shot them down one by one. Anyway, it seems the last of the Italian dudes said that she must truly be a princess after she told him to fuck off right there in front of everyone. From that moment on the Italians called her Princessa." Dave Lohr paused for a moment to eat some cheese. "Elaine really is low maintenance, man."

"What do you mean? Craig Rose asked.

"She's an old soul … traveled a long way to get to where she is."

"Where is she?"

Just then they heard her shout as she came back up over the rise to join them. "About fifteen more minutes boys, then we gotta go." Dave Lohr did not have time to answer the question.

They obediently put their belongings back in their packs and prepared for departure. The climb was becoming even steeper and the air cooler with the altitude. In another hour, they would be above timberline.

"You guys given any more thought to doing the Complete Ridge?" Dave Lohr asked.

They hiked for a few more steps before Hempstead answered, "We're split," he said. "I'd like to give it a go, but Craig wants the summit before we trump-up the route."

"That was our goal, wasn't it, Jim?" Craig Rose was defending himself and not too subtly hinting at Hempstead to help put an end to any further discussion of the Complete Ridge.

"Look," Elaine said, "we've got two guides, two routes, and apparently two goals. I have a solution. Craig can do the Upper Ridge with Dave, and I can take Jim up the Complete."

Jim Hempstead was clearly on the spot. He too wanted the summit badly. He knew that attempting the Complete Ridge greatly diminished the likelihood of a successful summit bid. He thought about how he and Craig Rose had come to climb together, but it was now more important to him that he not disappoint Elaine. He tried to pull Craig Rose to the side in an effort to speak to him.

But he didn't give Hempstead a chance. "Hey man, if you and Princess Yoko want to climb alone," he said loud enough for everyone to hear, "then please go right ahead."

There wasn't any thought involved. He stood there for only a moment before he said "sounds good to me," and committed himself to the Complete Ridge. For the first time on these trips, he and Craig Rose would part company --a violation of the unspoken code existing between them.

There was no more talk as they approached the gravel moraine generated by the glacier. The water flowing at the bottom was a milky-white color as a result of the pulverized rock and stone that it carried away from the glacier. Their breathing became more difficult and it was hard for them to get sure footing on the steep gravel grade. Hempstead struggled to keep from twisting an ankle or falling to his hands and knees and the effort was wearing him down.

Above them and still another hour away was the giant rock headwall that separated the glacier from the tundra saddle that sat between the Grand Teton and the Middle Teton.

When they reached the headwall it was getting very cool as the sun had faded westward behind the ridge. They took turns climbing up the fifty-foot, icy-slick rock face assisted by a thick fixed rope. When they were all secure above the wall, they hiked about four hundred yards up to the hut where they would spend the night.

The hut was located in the tundra at the top of the saddle. It was a tan barracks-like structure constructed of plastic reinforced canvas. It slept twenty people --ten comfortably-- and had a plywood floor that was stained from the wet feet and spilt meals that it had endured throughout the climbing season. The air inside held the stale smell of boiled noodles and mildewed sleeping bags.

Outside to the west they could see well into Idaho. To the east laid the entire expanse of Jackson Hole. As the sun further set, the granite peaks rapidly took on the familiar orange alpine glow.

Each climber became situated in their own space in the hut. They had been at it for over eight hours and they were tired. Doug Lohr was inspecting equipment while Craig Rose was putting on warmer clothes. Hempstead just sat inactively on his sleeping bag staring at his outstretched feet. He knew that the altitude was getting to him and yet he sat helplessly unable to care for himself. The thought of food and water made him ill and he began to feel the chill take over his body.

"You really need to eat, Jim." Elaine noticed his discomfort. "Come on, I know the best seat in the house. Let's go eat and talk about what's going to happen tomorrow. I'll point out the route."

She led him back down through the soggy tundra to the headwall and a cluster of rocks. They sat with their legs overhanging the wall. Down on the valley floor they could see the saw-tooth shadows cast by the Teton range.

She then turned her attention to her business. "All right, we're going to get up at one thirty," she said. "It's going to be a bright moon, so we probably won't need headlamps. We'll summit and get back to the hut well before the noon rains come with the lightning." She pointed out the route. "We'll need to move fast, but with just the two of us, we should be fine."

"You really don't sleep, do you?"

"In the mountains, there usually isn't time for sleep. You learn that night is just the other side of day, just like you learn that cold is just the other side of warmth." Elaine carved some cheese for Hempstead and forced him to drink more water from her bottle. "You know your buddy Craig didn't seem too fond of my plan today."

"He'll get over it ... especially if he gets to the top."

"I understand," she said. "So why do *you* do this, Jim?"

He thought for a moment before deciding to give her the easy answer. "I'm not really sure," he said, "I just know that when I climb, for that little bit of time everything is simple ... it's black and white and I like that feeling."

"What does your wife think about all this ... simplicity?"

"She thinks I'm self-absorbed and wasting money. It's amazing how people can grow so far apart. Neither of us is the same person that we were when we were married, and neither of us likes the person the other has become."

"Why don't you just divorce her?"

"My son. I don't want to hurt him."

"And you think he's learning how to love by watching the two of you?"

"I know, it sounds like an excuse."

She forced him to eat and drink again.

"Are you a good lawyer?" she asked.

"Now that's a loaded question. I don't know how to answer it."

"How 'bout honestly."

He thought for a moment. "Yeah, I'm a good lawyer--a damn good lawyer, which makes me bad, doesn't it?"

"I don't know, you're the lawyer."

"I'm good, but I'll never be a success."

"What do you mean?"

"I've always been afraid to just jump into the pool."

"The pool?"

There was a mocking look about her face and yet he knew that he had irrevocably committed himself to the discussion.

"Yeah," he said matter-of-factly. "The pool that washes people of human compassion. I'm unable to participate in any game where you keep score with money. So measured in those terms, I'll never be successful."

"You're so dramatic aren't you? It sounds to me like another excuse ... or you're a martyr."

"Whatever. But I believe most monetary successes are borne out of those waters. I've seen people lust after money and 'the deal' in a way that should be reserved for the opposite sex. I can't get there."

She kind of chuckled to herself. "I think I know what you mean. My aunt and uncle basically raised my brother and me. He had the most unbelievable natural skills in any sport that he played--I mean he was remarkable. Problem was that he just didn't want to do sports, ya know? My aunt and uncle were so frustrated. They'd say 'Why don't you play baseball? Why don't you play football? You're wasting your God-given talent.' I learned early on that just 'cause you decide not to play the game doesn't mean you can't or should."

Hempstead did not immediately respond. Elaine's openness had forced him to reevaluate her intent. "It's funny, the other night an idea came to me," he said when he finally spoke again. "It may seem ridiculous, but I thought about chucking it all and running away--starting an adventure travel company. Adventure trips for middle-aged people ... give them a chance to live for just once in their lives."

"I bet there's big demand. I bring a lot of folks like that up this mountain every year. Why don't you do it?"

"You sound like Craig."

"Why?"

"He thinks I'm plagued by having too many options in life."

"Damn, I'll think my life is coming to an end the moment I start losing my options."

There was more silence for a while as they both enjoyed the view and Hempstead forced himself to eat.

"Port Angeles, Washington." She did not offer any connection to their previous conversation. "It's the most beautiful place I've ever seen."

"Tell me about it."

"That's what happened around here--everyone told everybody else about it." Elaine was smiling. "All right," she said, "but you gotta promise not to tell. Port Angeles in on the northern most part of the Olympic Peninsula. It's a harbor village that sits on the Strait of Juan de Fuca. Across the water you can see Victoria, British Columbia. It's a wonderful sight on a clear night. The Olympic mountains drop straight into the town from the south. If you need the city, a ferry to Seattle is only about an hour or so away."

"Bet it rains a lot."

"Rain is just the other side of sunshine." There was a long pause. "Let's go, I know you like to go to bed early."

"You're never going to let me forget it, are you?"

She stood and pulled him to his feet. "Forget what?"

By then the evening sky was an surreal mixture of drab colors that Hempstead had never witnessed before. They

41

went back to the hut where Craig Rose was already in his sleeping bag. The wind coming over the saddle from Idaho started to blow hard and savagely buffeted the tent. Hempstead was determined to stay warm, so he put on all of his clothes before getting into his sleeping bag.

"Get some rest," Elaine said fastening the door to the hut. "You won't sleep like babies up here, so don't expect to. Just try to keep your eyes closed cause wake-up call is comin' fast."

Hempstead laid there listening to the wind batter the hut and Craig Rose peacefully snoring next to him. He struggled in vain to find some comfortable position that would send him off to sleep and fought off an increasing urge to go outside into the cold to relieve himself. If he was certain at all of anything in his life, it was that he hated having to pretend to sleep in the hut.

"Time to rock and roll!" she shouted.

The eternity of Jim Hempstead's night was over all too quickly. He had fallen into something approaching sleep at some point and he didn't want to leave it.

Even the liquid in their water bottles stashed inside the hut had frozen solid during the night and Dave Lohr was already up and boiling more water. He and Craig Rose had decided the night before that they would let Elaine and Hempstead leave first in the morning.

"Moon's out, wind's gone, and it's a wonderful night for a climb." Elaine's cheerfulness continued.

Craig Rose yawned and stretched. "What time is it?"

"One forty-five --we decided to let you sleep in," Lohr said adding coffee and oatmeal to separate containers of boiling water.

Jim Hempstead and Craig Rose started dressing themselves and when they were ready, they stepped outside into a morning as dark as the night before. It was cold and there was frost on the hut. A small shroud of clouds allowed most of the moon to shine down upon them, and Hempstead wondered how his freezing fingers could possibly grab the rock.

"Let's go, Jim." Elaine had a rope coiled over her shoulder and headed up the rocky landscape guided only by the moon.

As they started to walk, they heard Dave Lohr call out to them in the darkness. "Put your trust in Princessa, Jim. Have a good climb."

They hiked up the steep terrain for a long while before the silence was suddenly broken by a loud cracking sound.

"Rock!" she shouted. Elaine had kicked loose a bowling-ball size boulder.

He stood helpless and numb as the sparks cast by the descending projectile came toward him. There was a tremendous pain when it hit his shin.

"Are you all right?" she asked.

He tried to conceal the discomfort. "Just give me a second." The incident reinforced that bad things can happen suddenly, and he felt fortunate to have escaped relatively unscathed.

With a slight grimace on his face, he told her that he was all right and they began working their way up the moraine again. It was almost an hour before they finally reached the place where a rope became important. Hempstead was concentrating on the climb and his inability to breathe at that altitude and he had temporarily lost most of his concern for Elaine's beauty that had consumed him the day before.

"We'll rope up here," she said. "Look at that," she pointed off to the west, "you can see the lights of Idaho Falls, almost sixty miles away."

Hempstead thought for a moment about the thousands of people comfortably asleep in Idaho Falls oblivious to these two crazy mountain climbers peering down upon them like unnatural voyeurs in the night. Then he quickly forgot about it and began worrying instead about whether he would be able to see the handholds and footholds with nothing but the moonlight to guide him. Elaine secured their rope to their harnesses and checked to see that the carabiners were locked in place.

"All right, this first pitch is about fifty feet around this ledge. You won't see me once I get around it, so make sure you stay on belay until I signal you."

Elaine was careful to avoid stepping on the rope as she turned to begin her climb. She walked until the rope was tight between them and then stopped.

"On belay," Hempstead shouted.

"Climbing," Elaine responded.

"Climb on, Elaine," he shouted again, completing the familiar call between them that all climbers use as pass words for safety.

Elaine went into the night leaving Hempstead alone on the ledge. He kept the rope tight between them and his position secure. With the rope wrapped around his waist, it would serve as a break if Elaine began to fall. Even though he was not climbing, his belay responsibilities demanded his complete attention. It did not take long before the rope became taut.

"Off belay," came a shout out of the darkness.

Hempstead relaxed the rope and removed it from his waist. It was his turn to climb.

"Climb on, Jim." Elaine's voice was faint in the distance.

He moved along the ledge until there was nowhere else to go. Facing the rock, he began to climb. The footholds were good and the climbing relatively easy. In the dark, he could feel but not see the three thousand feet that separated him from the valley floor. He concentrated on climbing and quickly made his way to another ledge where Elaine sat waiting as she belayed him to safety.

"Excellent, Jim. How do you feel?" She was rapidly coiling the rope for the next pitch.

"That wasn't too bad." He wanted to sit for awhile and take in the orange outlines against the dark backdrop of the Teton range as the sun began to rise.

"We gotta keep moving. This next one might challenge you a bit more. If you stay to the left, I think the holds are a little better."

Elaine began to climb the pitch above them. As she climbed, he noticed her grace and ease on the sheer face. She moved like a cat prancing up the rock until she was out of sight again.

Soon, it was Hempstead's turn to climb again. As he did, he quickly ran out of footholds. It was getting a little lighter in the pre-dawn morning so that he could both see and feel the expanse that existed between where he was and the valley floor. He was pasted against the rock with nowhere to go.

"Mother fuck," he spoke to himself. As his limbs grew tired, his leg began to shake uncontrollably. Calm down, just fucking calm down, he thought. Push yourself away from the rock. He searched with his eyes and felt with his hands for a place to make his next move.

Seeing the slightest of protrusions from the rock above his left hand, he knew he had to go. "Fuck it," he scolded himself as he leapt for a new position. He reached it and held tight as his feet smeared themselves against the rock bringing him to the conclusion of this heroic move.

"You all right down there?" she called from above.

"Just taking my time," he said silently to himself.

When he reached Elaine again she could tell he was panicked and needed encouragement.

"Nice one," she said.

"Does it get more difficult?"

"We got a couple of tricky places above, but you're doing great."

Elaine turned and began climbing up the rock directly behind him. Jim Hempstead did not watch her. He studied the valley below looking for familiar landmarks as he belayed her. When it was his turn to climb again, the rock face was nearly vertical, but there were many excellent hand and foot holds. He was climbing confidently and soon reached Elaine at her belay point.

They climbed several more pitches and when the morning sun finally began to provide some warmth they took time to remove unnecessary clothing. Hempstead's fingers were ripped by the rock and bleeding but he ignored them and the mess as he changed into a lighter shirt.

"We're at a pitch called 'the Open Book,'" she said. "I'll have to belay you from a point that'll not be directly above you. If you fall, you're gonna swing back against the rock like a pendulum, so be careful."

As soon as he began to climb he understood how the pitch got its name. The rock wall was open vertically in the shape of a large 'V' that resembled a slightly opened book. He was climbing on the left side of the 'V', while Elaine was belaying him from the top of the right side.

The holds were good and he climbed quickly. He had forgotten all about the exposure and existed in a world that consisted only of himself and the rock directly in front of him.

Eventually he worked his way into a difficult spot with no apparent place to go. Thinking for what seemed to be minutes he finally wrapped his right arm around a small pinnacle of rock and reached mightily with his left leg so that it was completely extended in search of a hold. The side of his face was plastered against the rock scrapping it open. His next move was determined and swift. As his foot caught hold of the rock, he transferred all of his weight in that direction and proceeded with the hope that the foot would hold. It did. He had avoided the consequences of swinging back against the rock that he had just come from.

He was out of breath and exhilarated when he reached Elaine. "This is fantastic," he said, "but I need a break."

"We gotta keep movin'. We need to be off the summit before the lightning comes."

"Just gimme a couple minutes, all right?" He took some super glue from his pack and poured it into the slices on his fingers to seal them from bleeding.

During this respite, he began to concentrate again upon Elaine's beauty. This time, however, he was fixated upon her strength as an individual. She was taking care of him and he liked it. At that moment he fully understood what Dave Lohr was talking about when he said that Elaine was low maintenance.

"This next one is the crux of the climb," she said. "Take your time and concentrate. When it's done, it's a walk to the top." Elaine was in an obvious hurry to keep moving.

Hempstead's mind was quickly back in focus. He understood the crux of any climb was the most difficult part. She started climbing again, leaving him stranded there on his slight rocky perch where he lacked any freedom of movement and began to feel claustrophobic. There was no escape from his precarious position other than to keep climbing upward and he was glad when it was his turn to climb again.

The first couple of moves were relatively easy and uncomplicated. He proceeded to a crack in the rock that required him to twist his feet inside of it with each step to provide purchase for him to climb higher. At the end of the crack was a smooth vertical surface.

Jim Hempstead was climbing strong when his feet suddenly gave way without explanation. His heart became startled and he felt helpless as he fell in what seemed to him as slow motion. In that moment his thoughts became clear and unexcited. So this is how it happens, he thought. In that instant he understood how it felt to die and it was not bad.

At the moment that he had conceded to his death, the rope came snug jolting him back to life and breaking his fall. Elaine had just saved his life. He hung there thousands of feet above the ground and feeling more secure than he ever had in his life. In fact, he was inexplicably giddy with the notion of his predicament. It was all so simple. He began laughing hard like a child.

He eventually turned back against the rock and made his way up to Elaine shaking from the adrenaline that saturated his body.

"Almost there," she said not discussing the fall.

They scrambled up over an exposed boulder ridge and then traversed it heading north so that they were about one hundred feet directly below the summit. Hempstead was breathing loudly and could feel his heart heavily pounding in his chest. He watched her move in front of him with a confidence that removed even the slightest doubt that they would reach the top.

The boulders they were crossing eventually stopped at a smooth rock slab that was close to fifty feet wide and set at an angle of at least sixty degrees. Elaine paused and looked it over from top to bottom. The normal route was covered with verglas, a thin layer of almost invisible ice that makes climbing extremely treacherous.

"We'll have to cross this slab and then head up that rock over there that's been exposed to the sun to avoid the ice," she said pointing out the route. "I haven't gone that way in about three or four years. Keep me on belay until I get across."

That's great, he thought. He securely stationed himself and when he was ready, she walked across the slab as if she were a child walking a painted line on a school yard playground. Safely on the other side, she braced herself and called out for him to come join her.

His leg began trembling the moment he put a foot down on the pitch. If he slipped now, the best he could hope for was to swing back forcefully against the rocks about forty feet lower and on the other side. His breathing became short and rapid as panic took him over. He briefly turned against the glassy-smooth face in a futile search for some minimal handholds. Finding none, he realized that the only thing keeping him from slipping into the void below was roughly four square inches of rubber on the balls of each of his climbing shoes clinging to the rock. Put your trust in the shoes, he thought. Keep your weight on your feet.

Just as he was becoming concerned about sparing himself from the indignity of another fall --this time before her eye-- he heard her calling out in support. He looked over at her calmly sitting and holding onto the life-securing rope.

There was absolutely no concern at all apparent about her and he knew then and there that he was safe and that she would give him all of the time that he needed with impunity.

There was more concentration involved in that moment than in any case he had ever tried in his life. Every bit of living that he had ever done flowed through to him and converged at that single place in time. Just at that moment some synapse fired within him and he cast himself with a blind faith into the safety of her protective grasp easily walking across the rest of the pitch.

She let him sit on the rock beside her and catch his breath for a few moments before they moved on. Two more easier pitches and some bouldering led them to the top of the Grand Teton.

She put her arms around him. "We made it."

He tried to hold back the tears that began in his eyes. He had not cried since he was eight years old and he had no explanation for the source of them.

"You want me to take a picture?" she asked.

"No." It wasn't possible to take a picture of the mountain he had just climbed.

They hugged each other again and then sat silently at the top for a long while. The clouds from the west began to gather and sprinkle scattered drops of rain upon them. There was no thunder or danger of lightning and the sun behind the clouds assured them that the burst would not last very long. They just sat on top of the mountain and let the momentary rain soak them completely.

Elaine began to quietly utter syllables in rhythm. "Tum de dum de dum de dum dum … ."

"What song is that?" He asked looking at her and knowing that he was in a space with her well beyond that which he enjoyed at Colter's.

"It's not a song," she said. "It's a limerick my Uncle Billy used to say all the time. I like it when I'm happy and it makes me feel better when I'm sad."

"Are you happy now or sad?"

"I'm very happy."

"How's it go?"

She began reciting the poem:

"If there's one thing you should be learnin'
It's in the sun there is no pain.
So 'tis a wise and noble person
Who sees the other side of rain."

"I get it. Port Angeles, right?"

"Any place it rains, even now." She was staring out over the valley far below them. "It sounds corny, but life is a gift." She sat quietly for a moment more before she spoke again. "I believe that for a person to be truly happy, he must find something, anything, and give himself totally and without question to it. The only thing is you gotta be careful 'cause once you give yourself to something, you can never take it back ... then again, nothing can ever take it away from you either."

"And to what have you given yourself?"

"A celebration of the gift." She reached over and put something in his hand and said, "don't let anyone else tell you how to keep score, Jim."

He held the object up to his eyes. "What is this?" he asked.

She told him the story of the bullet and he put the band around his wrist. "Come on over," she said.

For the first time in his life, Jim Hempstead felt truly in love with another person.

They climbed down out of the rain and met Craig Rose and Dave Lohr who had been back at the hut for about an hour because they had a shorter distance to travel. After they all congratulated each other on their successes, they had a quick lunch consisting of cold bagels and beef jerky before beginning their long hike back down the mountain.

When they reached the end of the trail Hempstead was exhausted, dirty, thirsty, and hungry. It was difficult and painful for him to peal the socks from the blisters because his blood had dried sealing his wounds to the cloth. Removing

50

the soiled wraps from his feet forced him to torturously initiate the injuries all over again. During that process, Hempstead could not stop licking the salt from the beard that was forming over his lip--it was an entirely odd sensation for a person who had shaved virtually everyday of his life.

When they were both finally in sandals, they limped to the car and quickly finished all of the water that awaited them before they all drove to Moose Junction to eat and drink. Hempstead's more overpowering urge, however, was to take a shower and improve his appearance for Elaine, although he knew it didn't matter to her any more than her appearance mattered to him.

The little café where they sat overlooked the mountain they had just climbed. Although he could not admit it to anyone, Jim Hempstead was more exhilarated by his time with Elaine than by his climbing success. He was hopeful that it was not obvious to everyone. In fact, it probably wasn't to Craig Rose. He was busy ordering one of each of the appetizers on the menu and talking about how he was determined to finish them all.

"You guys want to head over to the Stagecoach?" Lohr asked.

"I don't know how long I'm good for after all this," Craig Rose said with a mouth full of food.

"Some good tunes tonight would hit the spot," Lohr continued.

"I'm up for it," Elaine chimed in.

"Come on Craig, let's go for a little while and celebrate." Even though the beers on an empty and dehydrated stomach had hit him hard and quickly, Hempstead did not again want to appear the lightweight.

Craig Rose reluctantly got up to join them acting like a night of drinking would be some sort of burden. As they all left the café, Elaine grabbed Hempstead by the hand and held him back sufficiently long enough to separate them from Craig Rose and Dave Lohr.

"Come with me," she said.

"To the Stagecoach?"

51

"Just come with me."

She drove them in some form of ancient and rusted car that was not familiar to him. The music from the radio was filled with static and it did not take long before her hand slid from the gear shift to his seat. He did not hesitate in reaching for it. The sky was just beginning to turn dark as they moved toward her cabin.

Elaine lived in a two-room cabin in the wilderness that lies beyond Colter Bay, on Jackson Lake. She leased it from the United States Forest Service for a nominal amount in exchange for her willingness to serve as a volunteer fire fighter should the need arise. The cabin featured a large stone fireplace that she kept lit even during the summer months. When they stepped inside, she started building a fire and asked Hempstead to bring them each a beer.

After the fire was going, she picked up a stack of compact disks and began shuffling through them. She held one of them up in his direction. "Do you like The Smashing Pumpkins?" she asked.

"Only when I was young and only on Halloween."

"Oh, I bet you're the first person to ever say that."

She put on the music, which was the product of the only electronic device in the premises apart from the refrigerator.

"I do like the music," he admitted.

"Men are much better at writing songs about the women they lose than they are at holding on to the ones they have."

"Is that a chink in your armor?"

"Kiss me," she demanded as she pulled him close to her body.

The sanctity of his marriage was now universes away and belonging in another lifetime. She pushed him slightly away and without taking her eyes from his began to remove each article of clothing. She stood silhouetted before the fireplace and began to move to the rhythm of the music. He moved closer and they began to dance palm-to-palm and skin-to-skin.

When the passion was more than he could bear he grabbed her by the waist and tried to pull her to the floor.

"You're not too old are you?" she chided.

"Fuck you."

"I thought that I would, but not here." She took him by the hand and led him outside. "Look up," she said.

The night was ablaze with a wondrous celestial show. Shooting stars from a meteor shower filled the night sky. Off in the distance the moon gave light to the contours of the jagged Teton range. Against that backdrop, Jim Hempstead made love with Elaine Sutter in a manner and with a feeling that he had never had with any person before.

She rolled him over then bent down to whisper, "so how's it feel?"

"How does what feel?" he smirked.

She was rubbing the muscles of his bare shoulders and her working fingers sent warm and indescribable impulses of caring throughout his body. No human should go through life without feeling a touch like that and he had waited over half of his life to experience it for the first time.

"You're married, you have a son, and you just made love to me under the stars," she said.

"I am home," is all that he could say.

Chapter 3

"May I see a wine list?" Keith Warren asked the waiter.

He and Diane O'Rourke were having their first lunch together. She was a stockbroker's assistant in his office, but had always avoided Keith because she was married and had heard the stories.

"I'm glad that you will be able to help me with Patton," he said, wanting to reconfirm the purely business nature of the lunch. Keith had convinced Diane that her invaluable assistance might help him land the William C. Patton investment portfolio.

"I'm flattered you asked," she said, "but just what exactly do you need me to do?"

"Right now, you can tell me what your preference is for wine."

"I don't drink wine at lunch. You know Patton has fired his brokers at Demmond and Associates, and I think..."

"I'm not asking you to drink wine at lunch to get drunk," Keith interrupted. "I just believe that a fine meal requires a fine wine complement."

"I agree, but this isn't supposed to be a fine meal. I'll pass on the wine. Now,...."

"Well, don't you agree that anything that is worth doing, is worth doing right?" he interrupted again.

"I'm not stopping you from having wine, Keith. I don't want any, and I'd like to talk about Mr. Patton."

"Are you always in such a hurry?"

"I only have an hour for lunch." Diane was now certain that everything she had heard about Keith and women was true. "I think that we ought to have Patton in and show him what we've done for Mr. Zaks and Mr. Springer."

"Good. Will you put it together if I get him to bite?" He said hoping that their business was concluded.

"I have no doubts regarding your salesmanship," she said. "You get him in, and I'll have your show ready."

They finished their lunch and left for the office--but only after Keith had finished his wine.

Keith Warren had caught his wife with another man eight years, three months and two days before his first lunch with Diane O'Rourke. As punishment, he never bothered to get a divorce. Instead, he became consumed by his own extra-marital affairs. He had learned that married women were, by and large, lonely women, and his virtually unanimous reward for some time and attention was a secret physical relationship. The more the better. Keith never fell in love with these women and felt little need to restrict himself to one relationship at a time.

He became a student of sex. From the Kama Sutra to Tantric Yoga, Keith took Eastern techniques for enhancing sexual pleasure, freed them from the attendant spiritual burdens, and turned them into power with women. To the extent that it was in his best interest, he paid attention to the women he was with and put their needs first. A number of the married women that Keith had been with had not experienced sexual pleasure before Keith. Certainly none of the women had experienced sex the way that they did with Keith.

The only apparent consequence of his escapades was the development of a Pavlovian-like response to ringing telephones. He assumed that, regardless of where he was, if a phone was ringing, it was some despondent husband or jilted lover calling to ruin his life. The physical manifestations of that reaction were something to behold. A quick jerk of the head leading immediately to a nervous itch on the left forearm followed by a long sigh of relief when he learned that the phone was not for him. He heard phones ringing everywhere. He began hearing phones that nobody else could hear.

Keith was so obsessed by telephones that, at night, after his wife would fall asleep, he would ritualistically unplug all of the phones in the house before going to bed. He would plug them back in before he left for work in the morning. Keith truly had a phone problem. And for good reason.

He had received many bad telephone calls. Just as he had learned to conquer married women, so too had he learned to conquer their husbands. He mastered the ability to convince them that they were the lone cause of their wives' affairs. He would tell them simply that they should have paid more attention. It was remarkable the number of marriages that Keith had saved in this manner. It was also remarkable that it had never occurred to Keith that his own marriage had failed for the same reasons he could so aptly explain to others.

The note on Diane's desk the next morning read simply:

"Thanks for lunch. Looking forward to closing the deal." /s/ *Keith*

Chapter 4

Jim Hempstead had arrived back in Ohio by mid-afternoon. It was a typically hot and oppressively humid summer day and all he could think about was how he very much missed Elaine and the splendor of the mountains. It was not unusual for him to try as best he could to make up for his absences with feigned attention toward his wife so he had decided to take her out for dinner.

It was dusk in Cincinnati by this time and they were driving on the Parkway that follows the Ohio River heading for Mount Adams. The restaurant was high up on a hill overlooking the city and was as close to a mountain as Krissie Hempstead ever cared to get.

"I'm not feeling well, Krissie," he told her.

"Did you catch something on your trip?" Her tone let him know that if he did, he deserved it.

"No. I mean I'm not feeling too … happy, you know what I mean?"

"You need to grow up is what I think."

"Can't you try to be my friend and listen to me for just once? I think I need to see someone. I'm depressed and I want to talk to a shrink."

"You're just feeling guilty because you don't pay attention to your family."

"Would you be upset if I saw someone?"

"You've always done whatever you wanted, so go right ahead."

"You're so fucking compassionate."

"We've ruined our lives and now we're sentenced to one another. I've lost my compassion."

Jim Hempstead felt the rage rise within him and fought the compulsion to jump out of the door. What in God's name had he done to put him here? The remainder of the ride up the swerving road to the restaurant was quiet as Hempstead relived each blow of every bad word she had ever spoken to him.

He had reserved a table against the window so that they could admire the lighted bridges and buildings below them, and pretending to take in the view offered them ample excuse for not speaking to one another. They mechanically went through the motions of dinner. They had nothing left to talk about, and ate their meals without much further conversation.

Hempstead studied the coal barges going up and down the river. He mentally placed himself on the crew of one them and was excited about discovering all of the people, the docks, and the towns that he imagined existed along the way to New Orleans. He didn't care what Krissie was doing or thinking.

When they got back home, Krissie immediately went to get ready for bed. Hempstead walked into his son's room and kissed him as he slept. After a few moments, he woke him up.

"I want you to know how much I love you, Mikey."

"Love you too, Dad."

"Give me a hug."

He hugged his son long and hard.

"Remember, when you shake a man's hand, shake it firmly and look him in the eyes."

"I know, Dad."

"I want to give you something," he said and handed the boy his leather bracelet. "It's a good luck charm."

"Thanks, Dad. Can I sleep with it under my pillow?"

"You sure can. Good night, buddy."

He kissed his son and walked back into the bedroom where his wife was already in bed.

"I love you, Krissie."

58

"Turn the light off, please. I'm very tired."

Hempstead climbed into bed next to her careful not to let any part of his body touch hers. He had made up his mind.

When he awoke early the next morning, Hempstead was very methodical. On the kitchen table he placed his will, his insurance policy, and a letter he had written to his son.

He went back upstairs and woke her. "I'm leaving, Krissie."

"We were out late," she said. "Did you really have to wake me up to tell me that?"

"No, you don't understand."

She just rolled over to face the opposite direction and pulled the covers up around her shoulders.

Hempstead left for work well before anyone else could be expected to arrive at the office. When he got there the underground parking lot was empty and he retrieved a suitcase from the trunk of his car before taking a slow elevator to the mezzanine level of the building. Another elevator took him to his empty office on the thirty-second floor. In his top drawer was an envelope full of money. Hempstead had always cashed his expense reimbursement checks and stored the money in his office. That way, he never had to account to his wife for the money he spent. Over the years, he had accumulated about fifteen thousand dollars in his envelope. Also on his desk was a memorandum drafted by an associate attorney detailing the jury verdict in the case he had just tried. He did not bother to read it or even to learn of the result. He simply took the money and was gone before anyone had arrived.

Hempstead left his car parked in the firm's parking lot and walked over to the hotel that adjoined the building where he worked. Outside and in front he hailed a cab.

"To the airport, please."

"You got it. Going away on business?"

He didn't answer. He stared instead at the driver's picture on the license that was hanging over one of the

59

visors.   His name was Adedapa Ajaiyeoba.   Of course
Hempstead couldn't pronounce it but he did consider its
possible national origin. He wondered about the events that
might have brought his driver to this country and what this
seemingly happy person might have left behind wherever it
was that he had come from.

He transferred himself into the stories that his mother's
father had told him in broken English. Sitting in the taxi he
became his grandfather as a young man when all the men
living in his little village in the Macedonian mountains were
called to arms.   None of them wanted to fight.   Their
enemies one day would be their allies the next: why not just
wait? It was 1922 and he found himself flung into an army
organized to promote objectives that he didn't give a shit
about. He didn't even have time to marry the girl who had
been given to him.

It was not his army and when he ran away it took a
fortnight of traveling only in darkness to get back to his
village and to her house. He stayed only long enough to tell
her that if she loved him to meet him in Paris. He waited
there for her until she came.

They married in the shadow of the Eiffel Tower and he
took her immediately to the shipyard where he looked all
around until he found the person who looked something like
him. It didn't take long for him to do what was necessary to
get the man's papers --documents that were hanging on the
wall of Jim Hempstead's law office at that very moment.
With a new identity that he would carry with him until his
death, his grandfather departed for Ellis Island, with his new
wife leaving everything else in the world behind.

They worked hard in America. He was a laborer for the
railroad where they laughed at him because he couldn't
speak English. She toiled as a seamstress and raised their
two daughters. Eventually they scraped together enough
money to buy a little restaurant where they happily worked
for the rest of their lives.

His grandfather in later years spoke to Hempstead of the opportunities in America, and how all he wanted in the world was for his children and their children to have a better life than his. "If you want it, you gotta work for it, Jimmy," he used to say. It choked Jim Hempstead up to think about it and emboldened him to think about the man. He was doing the right thing.

When they arrived at the airport Hempstead was careful to hand the money to the driver over the back seat to avoid face to face contact with the man. He walked through the automatic doors and up to the counter.

"Like to buy a one-way ticket."

"Where to?"

"Seattle."

Krissie Hempstead didn't mourn her loss at all, if there even was one. She really didn't even bother to look for him or to make a big deal out of things. Instead, she focused tenaciously on getting what was due to her. Using the might available from his law firm, it was not difficult for her to have him declared dead and to collect the insurance money. Six months later, his partners finally filled his vacant office and were relieved to turn it back into productive space by placing a living and billing human being in it.

Krissie Hempstead had learned about that because shortly after the legal necessities were concluded, declaring her husband legally dead, she married the partner who had volunteered to navigate her through the process. She would tell everyone that prior to that time that she had only known who he was from meeting him at firm holiday parties over the years. How fortunate she was to get to know the love of her life at the time that she needed it most.

The stories about Hempsteads' disappearance were many and varied. Most people were certain that Jim Hempstead had committed suicide. But no one, not even Craig Rose, thought that he had it within him to simply run off.

Krissie never showed her son the note she had found on the table the morning that Jim Hempstead had disappeared:

My Dearest Michael,

I was gone from you long before now. Some will say that if I loved you, I could never have done this: they are wrong.

I have given to you all that I could constructively give, and I feared that my further example would have been the wrong example.

I am hopeful that, in time, you will come to appreciate my love for you. Please live your life and love yourself.

I love you,
Dad

Chapter 5

Diane worked hard preparing the Patton presentation. She was thirty-four years old and had completed all but her last year of college. Thinking that she was pregnant, she married without much consideration and never had the time to finish school. She was just as wrong about her pregnancy as she was about her marriage.

Patton had given Keith his current portfolio and in essence told him to "beat it" and the work was his. Diane took her assignment from Keith seriously. She gathered together the analysts and enlisted their input. Picking, choosing, and hedging among the multitude of industries, funds, and markets, she acted like some sort of peasant at an open-air market checking the produce. She meticulously put together a report complete with all the fancy computer graphs and charts that are so absolutely essential to lend credence to any presentation. This was her opportunity to succeed and she wasn't going to blow it. After weeks of round the clock effort, it was finally ready.

Now, he was in Keith's office pensively waiting for his response to her report. Keith intently studied its contents and then threw it down on the desk.

"This is fantastic," he said. "Do lunch, today?"

"I'm gonna get fat if we keep this up."

He put on his coat and searched for his car keys in a drawer. "I'll take my chances."

They drove for a long while and were well beyond any radius that would suggest a quick lunch.

"Where are we going?" He finally asked him.

"I know a little spot I'd like you to try in Springfield."

"But that's a forty-minute drive." She complained that, unlike him, she was an hourly employee and could not take extended lunches without consequences.

"It'll be worth it," he said. "Besides, it'll give us time to finalize the presentation. Consider yourself at work."

Keith was headed toward a restaurant called The Bard. It was an old country mansion converted into a restaurant. They were on a two-lane road with giant oak trees on either side growing together to form a dark green canopy over them. The sun was out and thoughts of the office were soon lost.

The wallpaper in the hallways revealed the restaurant as an antique. The paintings were of faces that had perished well before the twentieth century. They walked past several larger dining areas and were seated in a small wood-paneled room where they didn't recognize anyone. There weren't many other tables around them because the large oak bar that serviced the entire of the restaurant commanded most of the space. All about them was the sound of the old wooden floors creaking as the waiters went about their business.

He ordered a bottle of Opus One. By this time in their relationship, he had convinced her of the suitability of wine at lunch. They had also grown to know each other a little better. That is how he knew there was something that she was holding beneath the surface and that was bothering her.

"What's wrong, Diane?" He asked pretending to look over the menu that he knew very well.

"What do you mean?

"You seem … if it's none of my business, then I'll shut up. You should be thrilled right now, that's all."

"It has nothing to do with work."

"All right, then, we don't need to discuss it. You've done an outstanding job getting ready for this thing tomorrow and if it goes, it's cause of you."

She was staring at the menu. "Glad someone thinks I can do something right."

"What's up, Diane?" He knew what was up.

"Joe thinks I'm working too much. He wants to have a kid, but I'm just not ready. There's a lot I want to do with my career first."

"You keep it up like you did with Patton and you'll do just fine. Take control of your career, Diane." Empower her, he thought.

"Thanks. I really didn't want to talk about a personal issue. Sorry."

"I'm the one who asked. You can talk to me anytime about anything. Do you want to have kids?"

"In order to have kids, don't you have to have ... " there was a pause, "someday, I guess, just not right now." She nervously swirled the ice around the cusp of her water glass.

"You're doing a great job, let's just eat and enjoy. If there is anything I can do, let me know." He reached and filled her wine glass. He was now certain that she very much felt alone in her marriage.

"He doesn't love me, Keith."

"I'm sure that he does. Everyone has their issues, you know?"

Diane became lost in the moment and the attention. She was becoming mildly disturbed that Keith had never shown more than an interest in friendship. She had heard the stories.

She pushed aside the dessert menu. "I bet I've put on ten pounds since we began working on the Patton stuff. No dessert for me today."

"They have chocolate mousse." He pretended not to hear her. "I think chocolate mousse is the most sensual food there is."

"I'm sorry, have we just changed subjects?"

"No. It's just an observation. Would you like some mousse?"

"I can't keep eating like this."

"The taste and texture of rich chocolate mousse in your mouth is worth the calories. Especially if there is the slightest touch of whipped cream involved." Keith noticed how her sweater teasingly hid the shape of her breasts.

"You want me to get fat?"

"The only thing better is to wash it down with champagne."

"I already had two glasses of wine, Keith."

He issued his directions to the waiter without seeking further approval from her. "We'll split a chocolate mousse and bring us a bottle of Domain Chandon Brut."

"So, you just take control, huh?"

Before he could respond, Keith's beeper silently buzzed in his pocket. He excused himself to make a telephone call. The phone was located down at the other end of the long hallway that they had walked through to get to the table. He dialed the number.

"I've got this lunch appointment, but when I get back, how 'bout meeting me for a drink?" He looked around to assure himself that Diane could not hear. "Yea, I miss you." He listened and smiled. "Me too."

When he returned to his seat the mousse and champagne had arrived. The mousse was perfectly placed in a single champagne glass with two long spoons set on the side of the plate. It was topped with just the smallest of dashes of whipped cream. She was waiting for him and had not yet begun to eat it.

"You must be pretty important getting paged in the middle of lunch," she said.

"Sometimes I think this instant communication business makes life more complicated rather than easier." He tried to deflect attention from his beeper. "Cheers," he said lifting his glass in her direction.

She took a sip of champagne. "Are the stories true?"

"What stories?"

"About you and women?"

"I'm married."

"I'm just asking."

"Look, my wife and I have our problems. I haven't slept with her in probably two years. But this bullshit about me and women offends me."

"Okay, but you can't blame me for asking."

"Cheers." He lifted his glass again. "Eat some mousse. It's meant for two."

On the way back to the office, Keith was thinking about how the drive was his favorite part of dining at The Bard. He enjoyed the uninterrupted time alone or with a companion. The sun was shining and he did not want to go back to work.

Diane was staring out the passenger side window. "I was hurt you know."

"What do you mean?"

"If the stories were true, I was hurt that you hadn't tried anything with me."

"Well, now you know the stories aren't true because if I were going to try something, it would certainly be with you."

Diane was amazed at what she had just said and wanted to retreat. "I didn't mean anything by my question, I was just curious."

"I know."

When they arrived back at the office they were quick to affect an appearance of a professional relationship but it was clear to both of them that the nature of that relationship had just dramatically changed.

Chapter 6

The goal of their business was simple and they were achieving it: live a life of adventure at other people's expense. In the short time since they had started The Adventure Company, Elaine and Jim had gone white-water rafting down the Colorado River, trekked across the Olympic Peninsula with a group of sorority women from the University of Washington, and followed the Pacific coast riding their bicycles from Seattle to Sausalito, California with a father and son attempting to overcome their dependency issues. They weren't ringing any financial bells and were essentially living a hand-to-mouth existence. But that didn't matter at all to them.

They had rented a small inexpensive cottage that had only two rooms. There was a bedroom and a larger living area that also served as a kitchen. But their home sat right on the water and the window just above their stove offered an ever-changing and eternally gorgeous view overlooking the water. Hempstead found Port Angeles to be just as fantastic as she had described on the mountain.

It didn't take long for them to fit neatly into the quiet little community. They were also a well-suited pair for their enterprise. Hempstead had the ability to monitor their minimal financial and legal affairs. Elaine was responsible for planning, implementing, and guiding all of the adventures. Neither intruded, or had any desire to intrude, on the other's territory.

After running about six miles or so along the coast line very early in the morning, Elaine had left to go attend to some errands. Hempstead killed the time bringing himself up to speed on her music and reading Hemingway while lying in a little hammock strung between the pillars of their back porch. There was a magnificently wonderful breeze blowing in off of the water and he only wished that he had his own music to listen to some of the time.

"Denali," was the first word from Elaine's mouth as she walked in the door. She had a bottle of wine with her and some swordfish steaks for the hibachi grill that they kept in the little bit of a grassy area that they maintained just off the porch.

He set his book down and got up from the hammock. "Looks like we're celebrating. What's up?"

"Denali ... Mt. McKinley ... three rich investment bankers, and the climb of our lives."

"Is that all?"

"Is that all?! Have you lost your mind? Babe, you and I are going to Alaska for three weeks to climb the highest mountain in North America all paid for by three wannabe climbers from Chicago."

"Three wannabe climbers whose asses you'll have to haul up that mountain."

"Start gettin' in shape, honey, we're goin' to Alaska."

"How'd this happen?" he asked.

"Got a call today from Paul Whittaker. He said these guys applied for his trip about a week after it had filled. He gave 'em my name. They were interested and Paul and I called them back together. That's where I was. I didn't want to say anything until I knew for sure. It's a done deal, Baby. Three guys willing to spend fifteen thousand dollars each for the luxury of spending almost a month eating, sleeping and shitting on a mountain."

He followed her into the kitchen. "You sure know how to show a guy a good time," he said messaging her shoulders as she opened the wine.

"Fuck you."

"Thought that I would."

"No time like the present to start gettin' in shape." She reached behind and pulled him close. "Tum de dum de dum de dum dum ... "

With the new adventure, their lives would be full for at least the next four months. They would need to increase their exercise, coordinate permits, and arrange travel plans. The Chicago contingent had promised to send a $10,000 deposit, which would cover their living expenses in the meantime, and help them shore up their equipment list. Their clients didn't know it, but Jim and Elaine needed to buy a lot of winter climbing gear.

They forgot for a while about the swordfish but not about the wine.

Chapter 7

The presentation went extremely well. Richard Patton was comfortable that Keith Warren ought to be his new investment advisor. Diane was not in the room when it happened and Patton didn't even know who she was. But if the markets continued to grow, the work she had done on the account would yield Keith six figures a year.

He walked into her cubicle to share the good news. "You and I are celebrating tonight."

"Can't," she said. "Joe's taking me out to dinner. Says there's something he wants to discuss."

"Well, discuss it with him tomorrow, we're havin' fun tonight."

"I can't, but let's do it tomorrow."

"Suit yourself, but I'm at a loss to find a friend to celebrate with me this evening."

"I know, but I can't blow Joe off."

"You did an excellent job, Diane. I just wanted to thank you."

"Thanks. Let's do it tomorrow, all right?"

"Sure thing." He turned to walk away and Diane called him back.

Her laugh was transparent. "Did you even tell him who I was?"

"He'll get to know you," he said. "Believe me, he'll get to know you."

Keith left the office secure that he had earned his keep for the day. He drove to Novak's for some whiskey and a cigar. Novak's was a bar on the top floor of a renovated building in the art district. People were accustomed to seeing him there when good things happened to him.

The voice from behind the bar boisterously called out "What's happenin' Keith?"

"Hosed down a rutabaga today," he said, "and I'm feeling like some single malt." "Your call, buddy." Even after all the years he had never bothered to learn his friends' name.

The bartender poured the scotch on ice to let it chill. "How big a deal?"

He held his glass up to toast the air. "If it works out, would more than pay the rent."

His nameless friend reached under the bar to a private humidor. "Savin' this one for a special time. Enjoy!"

Keith grabbed the Cohiba and rolled it between his fingers before sniffing it from one end to the other. He knew his cigars. Not only a Cuban, but one of Cuba's finest. When the scotch was properly chilled, he lit the cigar and was feeling relaxed and pretty good about himself.

When the cigar eventually burned down to a mushy little stub, he twisted the remnant into an ashtray and left Novak's. As soon as he was in his car, he started working the phone.

"Hey, haven't seen you for a long time. Dinner tonight and see what happens?" He did not want to be alone.

Diane did not have an opportunity to go home first. She met Joe at the restaurant that he had chosen. It was one of those chain establishments that featured unique California cuisine. They rarely ate together and their dining habits were understated and understood. He would not even consider an appetizer or wine.

Diane had learned much about Joe's culinary inadequacies from her time with Keith. When she saw him sitting there waiting for her she immediately regretted that she had turned down Keith's invitation. They ordered dinner and were awkwardly awaiting its arrival. As they sat there she thought to herself that Keith would not be caught dead in this place.

"So, you said you had something that you wanted to talk about." Without waiting for a response, she motioned for a waiter. "Would you bring me the wine list, please?"

"Yea. I guess I'm feeling really distant from you and I want to know if there is something going on that I should know about."

"Not that I can think of."

"You've been spending a lot of time at work and coming in late. I'm concerned that you're putting work in front of our relationship."

She held up the wine list to him. "Would you like some wine?"

"No, thanks."

Turning to the waiter, she ordered a glass of Chateau Montelena. "I'm growing at work, Joe, and I like what I'm doing, that's all."

He looked at her as if he was surprised that she would even know how to order wine by name. "You're putting work in front of us, Diane. You need to spend more time at home. We should think seriously about children."

"I'm not ready, Joe."

"I want you to quit your job. I can take care of both of us."

"I'm just starting to get going at my job, I can't quit now. I don't want to. Why don't you quit your job?"

"You're making choices here, Diane."

"So are you."

He stood and threw his napkin on the table in apparent disgust. "Here's my credit card. I'm leaving. I want you to think about it. If you can't make this token commitment to me, then we need to think about where we are."

"There's nothing token about quitting my job."

"You heard what I had to say." He walked away from the table at the same moment that their meals were arriving.

Diane called him back.

"Yes?" he said.

"Here's your credit card, I have my own."

When she was certain that he had truly gone, Diane had the meals wrapped to go. She explained to the waiter that Joe had gotten sick and that they had to leave. When she got in her car, however, she called Keith Warren's beeper.

It began buzzing on the dresser next to the bed. Keith recognized Diane's number and was surprised that she would be calling. Normally, he would have avoided the page, but he was concerned that something might be wrong with her. He got out of the bed and went into the next room to return her call.

"Sorry to hear about Joe. Sure, I'd love to meet you for a drink, but I have a few errands I need to run first. How 'bout The Metropolitan Grill at nine o'clock?"

Keith came back to the room where the woman was still waiting naked on the bed.

He sat down and bent over to kiss her. "I love you, Honey. I'm sorry, but I've got to go back to work." He stood again and started to put his clothes back on.

"What is it Darling?" The woman was concerned and frustrated.

"Patton stuff, I've got to go."

She began pulling at the tail of his untucked shirt. "Will you marry me? Do you know how much I truly love you?"

He continued putting his shirt into his pants and she was forced to let go. "Of course I'll marry you. I'm gone for you, don't you know it? Just gotta let me work out my divorce."

"Just checking. Coming back? I want you to come back."

"Probably not. Let's do dinner tomorrow, all right?"

"Sure, I'd like that."

He kissed her on the cheek before he left.

Keith arrived at the Metropolitan Grill twenty minutes late. Diane was already at the table and had ordered a bottle of wine.

She lifted her glass. "Congratulations on Patton."

"You're the one that did it. How's Joe feeling?"

"He's pretty sick."

The waiter brought them menus. Keith picked his up briefly and set it down.

"I've got an idea. Anyone can have dinner in a nice restaurant. Let's just do dessert. It's a nice warm evening and we can drive down to the river. I know a nice spot to relax and watch the boats." Keith understood that the invitation would bring either an instantaneous rebuke or a welcome acceptance. But, after all, she was the one who had called him.

Her reply was instant. "Sounds like a lovely idea."

By the time they finished their dessert, Diane had drank more wine than she was accustomed to drinking. Her guard was down and Keith knew it.

"Let's just take my car. I can drop you off here on the way back." He did not even look at her for a response.

The top was down on Keith's BMW convertible. The warm breeze hit them as they drove along the road that wound by the river. The lights from the homes across the river reflected on the water as they made their way out of the congested city and into country.

"You won't laugh, will you?" she asked him breaking the silence.

"Laugh about what?"

"Joe laughs," she said.

"He laughs about what?"

"When he comes, he laughs."

Keith turned and looked at her but she was staring out the passenger window and he tried to conceal his own laughter. This was comically bizarre. "What does he think is so funny about coming?" He asked letting go the slightest chuckle before biting his tongue.

"Nothing, I don't think. He has some sort of wire crossed in his head, and when he comes, it makes him laugh uncontrollably. Some sort of neurological thing. It's not real romantic and it always makes me question my ... "

"Sounds like Joe is the one with the problem, not you."
He was finished talking about her husband--it was simply too
weird no matter how many points it might get him with her
to continue the easy put down. Besides, he didn't want to
laugh in her face.

Keith pulled into a secluded picnic area at a place where
the river formed a large pool. He put jazz on his compact
disc player. For the longest time they were silent, listening
to the music, and enjoying the view. Little sail boats were
traversing the calm water, their images barely visible in the
moon light.

Keith spoke first. "I care about you, Diane. Are you all
right?"

The words were hard for her. "No, Joe and I are on a
collision course, but I don't want to talk about it."

"Fair enough, let's just enjoy ourselves."

"Can I trust you? I really need to be with someone that I
can trust." Diane was looking directly into his eyes.

"Trust me, Diane ... rule number one is that we will
always be friends."

Keith reached over and put his arm around her. There
was no resistance, so he proceeded further. He pulled her
closer to his body and placed his hand on her lap. There was
still no resistance. He began rubbing her thigh and
messaging her muscles. She was receptive and he pulled her
head toward him and playfully kissed her on the mouth.

She reached over and frantically tried to unbuttoned his
pants. The signal was clear. He pushed her away long
enough to reach over to unbutton her pants and pull them
down around her shins. When he looked down it did not
take long for him to yank her panties down to the same
location. Keith proceeded to touch, feel, and lick her
completely. He tasted every inch of her body that was
exposed. He wrestled with her shirt until she volunteered to
remove it herself. Before long Diane was completely naked
in the front seat of the BMW. He continued tasting, licking,

and probing until Diane was frenzied. She was breathing hard and reached to pull down his pants.

Keith stopped her hand for a moment. "It's not a goal for me. You need to know that I'd much rather have sex than have an orgasm."

"What are you talking about?"

"I enjoy the circle of joinder created by two human beings making love. Why would I want to end that with an orgasm? Anyone can have an orgasm."

"What?"

"I'd rather be in you than come in you."

She reached over and pulled him on top of her even though he was still fully clothed. He kissed her as if butterflies were fluttering on her lips. His tongue was gentle and caring.

"Please, let me taste all of you," he said. "I want to take care of you."

He crawled down between her legs and grasped the seat lever lowering her in one movement. She relaxed in anticipation. He was soft and teasing at first. Her moisture flowed as she began to move in pleasure. He became more aggressive and she responded. When it was time, she pulled his head against her and held it firmly.

"I love the way you taste," he said, indicating his willingness to do it again.

She pulled him up from the floor so that his lips could reach her mouth. "Kiss me," she said.

He took the opportunity to put new music on before he kissed her lips again. When he was ready, he pulled away to remove his clothes. The sensation of their first naked embrace overwhelmed Diane. She wanted him immediately.

"Slow down," he said. "I want to enjoy every second of this."

"Then, let me taste you."

Diane pulled him over catching his back on the emergency brake as she switched their positions. He ignored the pain. She tried to mimic the attention that had so pleased her..

When she was finished, Keith got out of the car and opened the trunk. Inside was a cooler containing a bottle of champagne and two glasses. He returned to the front seat and opened the bottle. He reached over and kissed her again on the lips. He poured the champagne over her breast and caught it in one of the glasses. When it was full, he carefully lapped up the residue from her breast. He filled the other glass from champagne flowing over her other breast and repeated the cleansing operation.

"We still haven't made love yet," was his toast.

They finished their champagne and deposited the glasses in the back seat of the car. Keith rolled on top of her and entered her without hesitation. She felt no different than any of the others, and yet he was fully aware that what she was at that moment ceding to him meant everything to her. When they were done neither of them moved. They lay connected in the darkness and the music for the longest time.

"Oh my God!" Diane suddenly pushed him away and covered both of her eyes with the palms of her hands.

"What is it?" He was startled.

"All I can see is my husband's face, my parents' faces, my relative's faces, his relative's faces--everyone's faces. This can never happen again."

"Was it that bad?"

"No, it was that good." She began putting on her clothing as she could locate it about the car. "Oh my God."

"Please don't feel guilty."

"I'm sorry, it's not you. I'm glad for us --it was great. I don't know if I can face Joe."

"You're not gonna tell him about this, are you?" He was preparing for another telephone call.

"I can't. That's just it. If I do, it's over and if I don't, our trust is over."

"Settle down, calm down and relax. We've done nothing wrong."

78

Diane was quiet. Keith knew she wanted to get home and out of his car. He drove her back to her car holding her hand along the way. He pulled up to her car at the restaurant and got out and opened the door for her.

Keith kissed her long and hard then looked in her eyes. "So, what are you going to do with me now?"

Diane got in her car and left.

"Joe laughs," he said to himself watching her drive away. Shaking his head in disbelief, he got into his car and hoped the phones would stay silent that night.

"Where have you been?" He was sitting in their living room in the dark when Diane arrived. Joe had not changed his clothes and was surrounded by empty beer cans.

"I don't want to talk, Joe. I'm tired and want to go to bed." She didn't pause as she walked to her bedroom.

"Where have you been, Diane?" Joe followed her.

Diane knew Joe. She knew that he was relentless when he wanted to talk. She knew that he would pester her all night, but she didn't want to talk. Not tonight. She needed to think about things. What would she tell Joe? She didn't want to make this decision in an instant. "I've been driving around, Joe, I'm tired and will talk to you in the morning." It was true, she hadn't lied.

"I want to talk now," he impatiently demanded.

But Diane couldn't talk. Not until she had decided what to say. She knew she had to leave or she would talk. She needed time. Just give me some time she thought.

"You gave me a lot of news tonight, Joe, and I don't want to talk until I've had a chance to think." Still true.

"What's to think about, Diane?"

"It's late, Joe. Let's get some sleep and talk in the morning."

"I want to talk now," he said sternly. "Where have you been?"

That was enough. She turned around walked by him grabbed her purse, and went out the door. When she got in her car, the phone instantly started ringing. She turned it off.

Diane drove to a motel and got a room for the rest of the night buying her some time to think as well as some more to explain. It was a cheap room that did not seem particularly clean. She briefly glanced at herself in the mirror that hung over the desk and then turned off the light to avoid the sight of herself.

She tried to push it all from her mind. Just get some sleep, she thought, and think about it in the morning. Think about it in the morning. She laid down but did not sleep. She could not wait until the morning to think about it. Not only had she cheated on her husband physically, but she shared his most private secret with Keith --it was not her secret to tell. Joe laughs, she thought. Joe doesn't think anyone else knows he laughs.

The light came quickly and Diane was tired. It was just after six o'clock in the morning, and Joe would not leave for work for another hour. She decided she would go home to shower and change when he was gone. In the meantime, she just laid there overwrought with guilt and coming up with a plan to deal with it.

Her voice mail was full of messages by the time she got to the office, most of them from Joe. There was also an urgent message from him written on a pink slip and left on her desk. Before she could talk to Joe, however, she needed to talk to Keith.

She went to Keith's office and shut the door. She had decided to sacrifice a concern for professional appearances for her greater concern that she might be overheard.

"That will never happen again," she told him. "We will not work together again and I can't talk to you again. Don't follow me or try to talk to me or I'll go to human resources, do you understand?" She turned around and walked out of Keith's office. He would not go to Novak's that night.

When she got back to her cubicle, she called Joe.

"Hi, it's me. I had to think about what you were asking me last night and you caught me by surprise. I just had to go off and think, that's all. Can we finish our conversation tonight?" She listened. "Good, I love you too, Joe."

Keith had darn well seduced her, and she liked the attention. But she concluded that there were certain things in this life that she would never have, and one of them was Keith or someone like him. She was married to Joe and was going to keep her commitment to him. To do so, she had to get Keith out of her life and Joe back into it. She thought she had gotten Keith out her life that morning.

Dinner was waiting for her when she got home. Joe had prepared steaks on the grill and bought a bottle of Chateau Montelena. It was not the same vintage that she had ordered the night before, but it was enough that he had bothered to try to remember what she liked.

He handed her a card and flowers. "I'm sorry, honey. I over-reacted yesterday."

She was amazed and relieved. "I'm sorry, too. I just..."

"Shh," he interrupted her. "Let's forget about it, all right? Go change while I finish cooking dinner." He handed her a glass of wine.

She hadn't lied and didn't need to. Joe had put himself back in her life and she decided to leave it at that.

"We need a vacation," she said after changing her clothes. "I feel like Mexico or somewhere else in the sun."

Chapter 8

The Chicago contingent arrived at Seattle-Tacoma airport on time. Jim Hempstead recognized them immediately. The three of them wandered off of the plane strutting with a bravado that sent him dangerously ominous premonitions. They were in their mid-thirties, were not wearing suits, and appeared to be in shape.

Mitch Geiger was the tallest member of the group. He sported shaggy blond hair and had a firm jaw line. From all the planning correspondence sent over the previous months, Hempstead knew that Geiger was an MIT graduate who had made his money at an early age by designing a computer program that hedged natural gas futures in a way that made big money for the investment banking firm of Jennrett & Samuelson. At twenty-nine, he was set for life and had matter-of-factly decided that mountain climbing would be his next accomplishment.

Ken Shepherd and Sonny O'Neil were two senior associates who had not disclosed that the trip for them was nothing more than a career move. They believed that spending time with Mitch Geiger climbing a mountain would somehow separate them from the pack and launch their careers into heightened directions.

There was nothing remarkable about Ken or Sonny, except for Sonny's flaming red hair atop his boyish and freckled face. The sight of Sonny's hair made Hempstead think for just a moment about Craig Rose, but that was from before and he did not allow himself to stay there.

The three of them had spent months training for the trip. They had climbed the stairs of their sixty-story building on a daily basis with loaded packs. They had read all there was to read about Denali. They had run countless miles culminating with a mediocre finish in the Chicago marathon. None of them, however, had ever climbed or understood a mountain.

Elaine held up the sign that said "Geiger," the agreed upon rendezvous name. The group approached them obviously delighted with the precision of their logistical connection.

"Elaine?" asked Mitch Geiger.

"You got it. You the guys who want to take on Denali?"

"That's us," answered Ken Shepherd.

She held out her hand. "Glad to meet you. This is Jim Hempstead." After he shook their hands she said "why don't we get your stuff and grab a bite before you check into your hotel?"

"You guys need some help?" asked Jim.

"Nah, we packed light," Geiger said picking up his bag and starting off after Elaine who had already turned to leave.

"Good," he shouted down the hallway after Geiger, "we'll be in the green Jeep Cherokee out front that looks like it's never seen a suburb." He was not the leader on this trip, but neither was he about to let Geiger treat him as irrelevant surplus. He and Elaine were a team and these clients better get used to it.

After they were situated in the Jeep, Elaine drove them north on Interstate 5 past the giant Boeing complex toward downtown Seattle. They could see the lighted buildings, and the ships of all sizes docked along the shore barely lit up by the last of the clear twilight sky.

"You guys like music?" She asked with her eyes still fixed to the road.

"Sure," came one of the voices from the back.

"Good, let's go eat, listen to music, and talk about the climb."

They did not yet know one another and were largely engaged in meaningless small talk as they made their way to Pioneer Square just off of the docks that sat on Puget Sound. She finally parked the Jeep in a large public parking lot under a bridge. It was dark, and the street was dimly lit and full of people. They could hear music coming from the many venues that gave life to the area. They also heard the sound of the ferry as it blew its horn signaling its departure for Bainbridge Island.

She led them to Michelli's, an intimate Italian restaurant near Pioneer Square, that was slightly removed from the traveled path. They sat down at a large red and white checkered table and everyone ordered drinks. After some time with their menu's, Ken and Sonny eventually followed Mitch's lead and ordered fettuccini with smoked Red River salmon.

When the waiter was gone, Elaine began to mildly lecture. "I suggest we enjoy ourselves tonight 'cause from tomorrow until I put you back on a plane we're gonna think about nothin' but the climb. No more alcohol after tonight either 'cause it will only dehydrate and distract you."

Ken and Sonny looked in unison toward Mitch Geiger as if this mandated abstinence was not part of the program that he had disclosed to them.

"Elaine," Geiger intervened, "we appreciate that you want to instill in us a respect for the mountains. Believe me, we all here understand the risks."

"Look," she said, "I know I may sound like a bitch, but you gotta understand. It's easy to say you respect the mountain at two hundred and fifty feet above sea level. It's another thing to act with respect for the mountain at over twenty thousand feet. I'm responsible for all of our safety-- that's why you hired us. I take that seriously and I want my clients to as well."

"Maybe you should explain to them about last May, Elaine." Jim looked encouragingly for her to continue. He thought that maybe the tale of the disaster of guided climbers dying on Mt. Everest might enlighten their view of her concern.

"Two of the best mountain climbers in the world, and very good friends of mine, died along with ten of their clients." Elaine paused for a sip of her beer. "All it took was a sudden storm and a lapse in judgment --not too uncommon with altitude. I don't want to have to ever explain to any of my clients' families why their loved ones didn't return."

"What happened?" Geiger asked.

"Too many people, not enough experience, and a failure to turn around at the agreed upon time. They had decided the day before that, no matter what, if they weren't on the summit by two p.m., they would turn around. They didn't. Over two hours after the turn around time, most of them were still making their way up. When the storm came, it was too late. It stranded them above twenty-eight thousand feet in hurricane force winds and wind chills approaching one hundred below. Seems that summit fever got the best of them. Had they followed their plan, they likely would have all come back."

"Well, we'll follow the plans," Sonny responded jokingly.

No one laughed.

"It's not just that simple," Elaine said. "I've guided a lot of people who think they want to climb a mountain and then learn that their bluster and blow can't get 'em up." She drank some more beer and listened for a moment to the music. "Denali is high and cold and you better be in shape. This is serious stuff, and I just want you guys to get it 'cause any one of us can get the rest of us killed, all right?"

That was all that needed to be said. Elaine was completely in charge. When they finished, they walked outside and could feel the cool breeze blowing in off of the Sound.

"Follow me boys," she called in a loud voice. "I love the music in Seattle."

Elaine took them to a bar where blues could be heard coming from within. They paid a five dollar cover charge and were each stamped on the hand with a transparent ink that provided them with a pass for the night into any of the other bars. Over the next several hours, she escorted them from bar to bar with a different genre of music available at each. Her clients enjoyed themselves and gained a respect for her that would carry them through the rest of the climb.

Their last stop was The Colourbox. It was so crowded that its human contents were spilling into the street. It was in between bands and the stage was being dismantled by one set of roadies and reassembled by another. In the meantime, music was loudly playing over the sound system. The Colurbox's dingy brick interior is home to many wannabe contributors to the Seattle's alternative music scene and its flannel-adorned patrons.

Suddenly, the people who seemed to be tuning the instruments and doing sound checks for the band broke into a song without introduction. The music was cutting and loud and their clients quickly became privately consumed in a drunken delight. Elaine and Jim sat together at the bar and let them explore it on their own.

"Well, honey, think those guys will stick it out?" Jim asked.

"We'll see tomorrow on Rainier. You know, this isn't like our other trips, Jim. Denali is serious and that's why I probably over reacted back there."

"I love you, Elaine."

She smiled and kissed him on the neck before getting up to look for her clients. She eventually found them leaning against the wall watching the band. She pushed her way through the crowd so she could speak to them. "We better go, we gotta get up early."

The street outside had become a nocturnal circus of characters and netherworld of activity and Jim sensed that none of them wanted to leave. He more than they could have understood the pleasure of their anonymous freedom and the reluctance to give it up.

When they got back into the Jeep, Jim's ears were still ringing from the loud music. The ringing continued all the way to the hotel where they all poured themselves into their beds.

Before long, it was the telephone that was ringing. The light had not even begun to make its way through the motel window and it was a while before anyone answered it.

"Hello?" eventually came Geiger's groggy voice.

"We leave in thirty minutes, so get the boys up and get ready, all right?" Elaine showed no sign of wear from the night before.

"Okay, all right, I'll get 'em up." Geiger hung up the phone and still wasn't certain whether he was at home in Chicago or somewhere else. He was certain, however, that the voice on the other end of the line was commanding his immediate participation. He rolled over and turned on the light mustering all that he had for the reveille. "Hey, it's time to get up!"

"My god, my fucking head won't let me leave the pillow. What time is it, anyway?" Ken Shepherd said before he rolled back over and covered his head with the blankets. "Call her back and buy us some more time."

"It's five o'clock. Get your ass out of bed. We're out of here in thirty minutes." After last night's lecture, Mitch Geiger was not about to negotiate with Elaine for some more time because of a hangover.

Before long, they were moving, but still hurting. They took their turns in the shower and were packed and ready in time to leave. They joined Elaine and Jim who were already waiting and drinking the free coffee in the motel lobby.

When they were all finally assembled, they piled back into the Jeep and began heading south on I-5 toward Paradise, Washington. The plan was to spend two days on Mt. Rainier working on snow climbing skills before departing for Alaska. The clients looked desperately, but the clouds prevented them from seeing the mountain. They could have been driving anywhere.

After a while they turned off the highway and drove along two lane roads and through the small towns built to serve the logging industry. They eventually reached Mt. Rainier National Park but, except for the twists and turns in the road as they gained elevation, there was still no sign of the mountain through the fog.

It was well before noon when they arrived at the Paradise Inn. The enormous wooden structure was built in 1917, and was set in the mountain's sub-alpine vegetation at about five thousand feet. It had a sparse interior and a gigantic foyer area with wooden trusses and pillars made from the large fir trees indigenous to the area. There was no heat in the building, except that generated by the fire that constantly burned in the huge stone fireplace. To one side of the lobby area was a small bar, called the Glacier Lounge that seemed to be full of climbers shouting stories to each other. On the other side was a large dining-hall style restaurant.

Directly across the parking lot from the entrance was an old guide house that served as the launching pad for virtually every climb up the mountain. Its steep chalet-style roof had protected it well through the years from the tons of snow that fell upon it each winter.

"After you get checked in," Elaine told them, "let's meet out in the lobby in about half an hour."

She took her eyes from them and waived to a man who was walking in with a group that had obviously just climbed the mountain. "That's Digby Whalen, one of the first American climbers to summit K2. Never know who you'll run into up here." She turned back toward her clients. "Anyway, bring a day pack with rain gear, your climbing harness, crampons, your ice ax and plenty of water and snacks."

Jim knew that Digby was a well-known Seattle lawyer who also excelled at mountain climbing. He was envious of Whalen's ability to openly incorporate into his life a passion for the law with a passion for adventure.

Perhaps sensing his preoccupation with Whalen, on the way to their room, she looked at him and said, "Whalen and I are just friends."

"I love you, Elaine," he said and just kept walking. He knew that she had had a life before she met him. He knew that on long climbing adventures, situations and convenient romances could easily arise and that she was not immune from them. He also knew that she had many friends that were men. Beyond that, he wanted to know nothing else. So when they arrived at their room, he simply picked her up, threw her on the bed and made love to her.

In the brief time they had alone in the room she was humming "tum de dum de dum..."as she changed her clothes. "Let's go see how much trouble these guys are going to get us into."

The three of them were standing in the lobby waiting in their new climbing gear and watching people come and go.

"What kind of snacks did you bring?" Elaine asked when she walked up and joined them.

Sonny O'Neil reached in his pack and proudly pulled out an assortment of flavored Powerbars.

"You know what happens to those Powerbars up high?" she asked rhetorically. "They freeze and you break your teeth trying to eat 'em. They'll do for today, but not on Denali."

"What will you take up McKinley?" Geiger asked.

"Plain baked potatoes, bagels, M&M's, and lots of rice, noodles, and tea. Jim and I will take care of the regular meals ... you guys figure out what you like to eat for snacks. Let's get started," she said.

Elaine led them to the dirt path next to the guide house. As soon as they started hiking the path immediately became steep. Her goal was to test their stamina so she intentionally picked up the pace and began marching them up to about eight thousand feet and to the Muir Snow Field. Her intention was to have them practice snow and ice climbing, especially belaying and self-arrest techniques.

The smell of fir trees filled the air and with all of their work, they really hadn't noticed that the clouds were lifting every so often, offering a glimpse of the summit. Before long, they were all sweating and breathing hard but Elaine kept up her relentless pace. If any of them was tiring, apparently none of them wanted to show it and falter or appear weak--especially at such an early stage. For his part, Jim was too busy trying to push thoughts of Digby Whalen from his mind to notice any physical discomfort. They took him over like a bad song in the middle of the night. With each step a syllable of that name came to his mind. *Dig, step, by, step, Wha, step, len, step, Dig, step, by, step, Wha, step, len, step.*

After just over a grueling hour they had worked their way to Pebble Creek and before much longer would arrive at the snow field. The trail leveled slightly at this point and Elaine brought her troop to a halt.

"Get something to drink here," she said. Pointing to the snow field about one hundred yards away, she told them that it led up to Camp Muir, the overnight stop for most people who climb the mountain. After they had taken time for some water she told them to put their crampons on and get their ice axes out.

They walked over to an outcropping of rocks that sat beside the edge of the snow and began securing the pointed steel-teethed crampons to their plastic climbing boots. She watched carefully because the last thing she wanted to do was have to help them put their crampons on and off while on Denali. To do so would take too much time and require her to expose her hands to the cold.

"A little tighter," she yelled to Mitch Geiger. "Those crampons have to become one with your foot." She walked down the row inspecting each of them. "When you've got your crampons on," she said, "I want you to check each other's out. We're going to be a team up there."

While they were doing that Hempstead helped her pull a rope from her pack and began securing each of them in place by their harnesses. In the midst of hooking them up Sonny accidentally stepped on the rope with his crampon.

"Bad play, man!" Elaine was loud and stern. "If you ever do that again, I'm not taking you up anything. This rope is our lifeline, and one misplaced crampon can cut it in two. I don't want to be on a rope that's been walked all over by someone's crampons." She picked up the rope from the snow checking to see that it wasn't damaged. Without close inspection, the nylon sheathing can close back over the rope concealing any damage.

Sonny's face turned as red as his hair. "Sorry," he said pitifully. "It won't happen again."

She didn't respond or apologize for her outburst.

The splendor about them seemed to diffuse some of the palpable tension. By that time of day the sun was really shining and radiating up from the snow. Off in the distance the Cascades still held snow up high, offering an invigorating view for many miles all around.

They spent the entire afternoon practicing self-arrest. Elaine explained that unlike rock climbing where one person is fixed and belaying a climber, on a snow and ice climb, groups of climbers are roped together and travel simultaneously. She told them that if one climber falls, the others must immediately dive face first into the snow and dig their crampons and ice axes into it serving as anchors and preventing the entire rope team from shooting down the mountain. Indeed, many an inexperienced rope team has suffered the fate of a single misplaced footstep--one person's mistake can be fatal to everyone.

She did not tell them that guides usually put the strongest climber in the back of the line to serve as the final bulwark against disaster. The second strongest climber usually assumes the lead position and the others are strewn in between. There was no need to start a competition between them.

She did tell them that when a climber begins to fall, it is incumbent upon him or her to yell "falling" so that the others will have a chance to go into self-arrest and belay the entire team. Those were the techniques that Elaine was drilling into her clients with a hope that they would become automatic if the situation required.

They worked in the snow for the rest of the afternoon until Elaine became satisfied that, with another day of practice, she would be willing to take them up Denali. At some point during their work Jim had managed to put Digby Whalen out of his mind.

When they were done, they hiked back down the steep trail more rapidly than they had hiked up. By the time they arrived back at the guide house, their clients looked totally spent from their day in the snow.

It was only four o'clock and they went directly to the restaurant. It had not yet begun to fill with the tourists who would take their dinner at a normal hour so they were able to select a table next to the window with a fantastic view of Mt. Rainier. It had completely emerged from the clouds and

91

loomed majestically in the sun. It was not lost on Jim that it would have been more than enough mountain for these beginners.

"Gentlemen, Denali's a go," Elaine said as soon as they all sat down. It was her first approving statement since they had arrived from Chicago. She lifted her glass in their direction. "'Denali' is the Athabascan Indian word for 'the Great One.' To the Great One," she said toasting them all.

None of them said anything, but Jim could feel the excitement and see the sense of accomplishment written all over their faces. At that moment he felt the disgust begin to well up inside of him again but knew his clients weren't to blame.

The whole situation was especially ironic. As a lawyer he had despised the governmental protection that was in such politically correct vogue. Law was enacted to protect people from themselves and everyone and everything else. Risk was no longer a part of the uncompensible equation. Stupidity could no longer be privately interfered with without cost or retribution--he had, in fact, vigorously defended a client who ultimately lost a several million dollar verdict to a woman who had spilled hot coffee in her lap while drinking it and driving at the same time. The jury had concluded that his client should have warned her that such a treacherous undertaking might cause pain. Yet, here were these people in search of the very thing that society would no longer let them have--danger with consequences and reward. He respected that. Maybe he wasn't alone, he thought.

As they ate their meals they talked and laughed about the many experiences that a single day in the mountains had already given them. And after a second day in the snow just beyond Pebble Creek, they were ready for the trip back to Seattle and the flight to Alaska.

Chapter 9

There was blood when Keith Warren brushed his teeth in the morning. The lining between the walls of his mouth and his gums appeared inexplicably torn open. He was confused but ignored it.

The first thing that he did at the office was get on a conference call with Patton, who was in New York. He found it difficult to speak the entire time. There was an irritation on his tongue that occurred whenever he tried to talk. When the call was finally over, he went to the men's room to look in the mirror. His tongue was littered with small white dots that were more than simple blisters.

Keith tried to think about other things in an effort to distract his attention from his oral disorder. Mostly, he thought about Diane. He had managed to avoid any contact with her. His ego was mildly disturbed by her apparent ability to easily cast him off, but he was nevertheless greatly relieved that there were no professional consequences resulting from their brief relationship.

For her part, Diane had done all she could to resuscitate her relationship with Joe. They sought counseling and then spent a week in Puerto Vallarta, where, of course, they both became ill and were forced to put any intimacy on hold. Nevertheless, she was determined to make it work with her husband, who remained oblivious to the affair with Keith.

Keith, on the other hand, was certain that her relationship with Joe would ultimately fail when the things that had caused her to look outside of her marriage in the first place inevitably surfaced. By then, Keith reasoned, he would have long been out of her life and would not be to blame for the certain demise of her marriage.

When he got home that evening, Keith locked himself in the bathroom and worked without success with a toothbrush and tweezers to rid himself of the growths that had taken over his mouth. He rarely saw a doctor, but made up his mind that he needed to schedule an appointment with one for first thing in the morning.

Chapter 10

Elaine, Jim, and their clients, arrived at the Anchorage airport by mid-afternoon. It took them a while to locate and collect their duffel-bagged gear from around the airport. While they did so, Jim left them to rent a van for the one hundred mile drive north to Talkeetna. Talkeetna was a small town that served as a hub for mountain climbers wanting to catch bush planes to the Kahiltna Glacier, which was the initial approach to any attempt at Denali.

Soon they were all riding in the van and listening to the music that Jim had selected from the tapes he carried with him in his day pack. The clients appeared to share his taste for Steely Dan's cynical lyrics while Elaine suggested that they were probably written in hieroglyphics.

Not too far outside of Anchorage the road became an obstacle course of potholes bouncing them all over the inside of the van. They all nevertheless seemed to be enjoying themselves except for Jim. For some reason he felt uneasy and could not purge himself of the non descript premonitions and feelings of doom that he was experiencing. He had never been on a mountain the size of Denali, and he convinced himself that his concern for the undertaking must be the source of his dread. So he sat silently and tried to enjoy his first ever view of Alaska.

When they arrived in Talkeetna, the small town was full of activity. It was a little outpost in the wilderness where the Chulitna and Talkeetna Rivers join the Susitna River and hold a bountiful supply of salmon and trout. What was once simply a stop along the Alaska Railroad had turned into an sportsman's outpost. There were bed and breakfasts, whitewater rafting guides, fly-fishing guides, hiking guides, and climbing guides.

They went into the Fairview Bar to have lunch while Elaine went to check them into their hotel. Mindful of her admonition back in Seattle, they did not drink beer, but Jim sure wanted to. Too bad he had to be with his clients and set some sort of example. Perhaps he could convince Elaine to join him there later that night after their clients went to sleep.

In the corner of the bar was a group of drunken Czechoslovakian climbers singing songs in their native tongue and celebrating their return from the mountain. The Fairview Bar seemed to Hempstead like Alaska's version of Rick's Cafe American-little clusters of climbers of varying nationalities all gathered together to this bar in the middle of nowhere and drawn by their common interest in climbing. Some were there drinking with the hope of a successful venture, and some were regaling themselves in the glory of their conquest. Of course, there were some that the mountain had simply thrown back to the Fairview Bar and who needed to console each other with the hope of better luck at another time. As he looked around and thought about things, Jim began losing his concern for the climb and actually began looking forward to it.

At about that time, Elaine walked up to the table and said "good news, gentlemen." She briefly glanced at a menu. "I've arranged for us to catch the first flight out of here in the morning." Over lunch, she described for her clients what was scheduled for the next several days and they appeared enthusiastic and eager to begin. "Eat well tonight and in the morning," she said. "And drink as much water as you can--remember, hydrate, hydrate, hydrate." She handed Mitch their room key. "When you're done eating, go lie down and rest. Jim and I are gonna' go and get some last-minute food supplies."

They listened to her and left. When she and Hempstead were finished with lunch, they spent the rest of the afternoon checking over the equipment and purchasing food rations at Nagley's General Store. Everything from food, climbing equipment, and medicine could be purchased at Nagley's, which would be the last place for them to purchase anything. Stocking up took them the rest of the afternoon and the last thing that they did was make sandwiches to take to their room for dinner. They were tired and needed rest. Jim did not suggest leaving for a beer, but he thought about it.

It was an old but clean hotel and their room was cool and dark. They lay quietly in their bed with the windows completely opened. The breeze blew in across them, bouncing their curtains against the wall to its rhythm.

He spoke softly and to the ceiling. "I had the strangest anxiety as we were driving up here today."

"If you weren't nervous about the climb, honey, you'd be crazy."

"I guess, but after this one, do you suppose we could scale it back a little?"

"Do you ever think about your family, Jim?"

He didn't immediately answer her. "I think about a lot of things, especially Mike," he said. "I want to write him a letter or call him to tell him I'm all right or just to hear his voice. Sometimes it kills me, you know? But I feel like the best thing that I can do right now is stay out of his life. Besides, if anyone figures out I'm alive, they may lose the insurance money. People must think I'm an asshole."

"What do you think you are?"

"God, it hurts. Why did you pick me, Elaine?"

"What do you mean?"

"You could have had anyone, you barely knew me, why did you pick me?"

"Because you want to be a child."

"So do all of the guys that exist in your world."

"But they are children, they were never adults. You were an adult and then chose to be a child."

"Would there be a difference if I had had no choice?"

"I love you, Jim." She rolled over and began kissing him. "We'll be freezing our asses off in a tent for the next couple weeks. Better take advantage of this opportunity, don't you think?"

"You know what I think."

"Just promise me one thing," she said.

"What's that?"

"When we get back, you'll call Mike."

He didn't answer her question. When they were done he feel asleep and dreamt.

Riding freely through a golden field on an auburn horse he effortlessly glided along as if being pulled by the rays of the sun. There were wonderful yet nondescript mountains surrounding the valley and the woman who rode along side had no face and no name, but she was him. There was no time and everything felt to him like it should when a crack of thunder shattered the illusion and behind him were countless angry tornadoes snaking down out of the suddenly darkened sky chasing them into somewhere he couldn't recall.

****

They were ready to go early the next morning. Their gear was neatly stacked on the small tarmac. The man who approached them appeared to be in his early thirties. He sported a five-day growth of beard, a torn flannel shirt and jeans. He took his sunglasses off for a moment revealing the permanent bags around his blood-shot eyes.

"You the folks going to Hotel Denali?" he asked.

"That's us," Mitch Geiger answered cheerfully.

"Well, I'm 'Diver Dan', and I'll be yer pilot."

Another nickname. Hempstead really was not too interested in learning why he was called "Diver Dan," and nobody else bothered to ask.

"How many trips do you think?" Elaine asked him.

Diver Dan reviewed the stacked equipment and turned and looked quizzically at his single-engine Cessna. "At least three, maybe four. It don't matter, I got the morning set aside for you guys."

"All right," Elaine said. "Jim and one of you guys will go first with as much equipment as safely can get on the plane. When you get to the glacier, you can start getting us ready to move while Dan comes back for the rest of us."

The plane was rigged with retractable skis under the wheels to facilitate take-offs and landings in the snow. There was a single seat in the plane for the pilot--the others had been removed to make room for cargo. They loaded as much gear into the remaining area as was possible before Jim and Mitch crawled in and tried to make themselves comfortable on top of it all.

Diver Dan started the engine and as the propeller jerked into action the whole plane began to shake and rumble. He turned and handed Jim the coffee that had been sitting between his legs before moving the throttle, that caused the plane to taxi down the tarmac before he abruptly swung it into position for take-off down the short runway. Without stopping or checking for clearance, Dan hit the throttle again and the plane began to accelerate and shake even more violently causing Hempstead to spill the coffee all over himself and the gear. He was not bouyed by the smell of the whiskey and coffee mixture. Just as the runway was about to come to an end, the plane began to lift easing, but not ending, the shaking.

When they were just above the trees and buildings, Dan reached for a cigarette. Hempstead noticed that his pilot's hand shook wildly as he tried to zero in on his target with a lighter. Probably the result of many an evening spent in the Fairview Bar, he thought.

The sky aloft was deep blue and crystal clear and the mountain ranges off in the distance looked fantastic. They were soon flying over clear-running rivers and deep green marshes full of moose, bear, and other assorted wild life.

"What do you think, Mitch?" Hempstead yelled over the sound of the engine.

He didn't respond and Dan held out two sets of headphones so that they could talk to each other over the turbo-charged noise.

When the plane finally leveled off, Diver Dan turned around and started talking to his passengers over his own headphone. He pointed out landmarks on the ground through the passenger windows not bothering to keep a hand on the wheel or to look ahead to see where they were flying.

When he finally turned back toward the front of the plane, he pulled suddenly back on the wheel, throwing the craft into a steep and sharp bank to the right and causing the maps, cigarettes and other tiny objects that Dan kept stored on the unintended dashboard to violently drop against the starboard door and then the floor as the plane eased back into position. They were flying between two peaks at a distance that Hempstead was certain would not meet with FAA approval and it scared him. Diver Dan told them that they were passing through One Shot Gap.

That's great, Hempstead thought, and he wondered who the losers were that perished wishing they could have had a second go at it.

Scarcely making it through the pass, Jim relaxed his sweating fist and caught his first glimpse of the Kahiltna Glacier far below. It appeared as a large white river of ice flowing for miles down from the mountain as the plane started to descend and follow its course. In what seemed to him like just moments after shooting the gap they were only several feet above the snow and making an unexpectedly smooth landing.

After coasting to a stop, Diver Dan left the engine running while they unloaded the gear. When they were finished, he swung the plane around and was gone without ceremony. The wilderness silence felt lonely to Jim as the sound of the plane disappeared. He immediately began stacking the equipment on sleds so they could haul it up the glacier to Camp One, but he could not ignore where he was.

Denali was an awesome sight. The massive geologic formation comprised nearly one hundred square miles. Hempstead thought that there was no way to describe the enormity of the mountain so that anyone who hadn't seen it could understand. It was an amazing conciliation for a person who had made a living explaining things to people

100

and he vowed to put those incomprehensible notions into words before he left.

The still distant mountain looked nearly vertical from their perspective and had a small silky band of innocent looking clouds just below the summit. The sun powerfully reflected up off of the snow and it was an amazing setting.

Just about the time that they had finished loading the two sleds, they heard the sound of Diver Dan's engine filling the sky again. Hempstead watched as it glided over the pass preparing to land on the glacier again. When it slid to a halt Sonny and Ken hopped out onto the snow. They stood gauking at their environment before they eventually took turns helping Hempstead unload more equipment. Within five minutes Diver Dan had swung around again and was gone leaving them alone again in the snow. The lack of formality in these departures really started to bother Hempstead. He was disconcerted at the apparent ease with which his pilot could so callously cast away such important relationships. Hadn't they just bonded in the air and become brothers in adventure? Not a sentimental fellow, he surmised. Or maybe they were not as important to Diver Dan as he was to them. Or maybe yet he was simply doing his job and that's all they had paid him to do.

In any event, Hempstead quickly realized that his analysis of Dan's psyche or motives was altogether irrelevant. There was no good reason to starting hating him too. He busied himself with preparing two more sleds with the gear deposited from the aircraft. While the others tried to help, their combined assistance actually created more of a nuisance than a productive effort. They were haphazardly stacking items precariously on top of the sleds so that, if he had not reworked it altogether, the gear would have continuously shifted about needlessly toppling the cargo about the snow.

"Why don't you guys make sure that you have on the right clothes for our hike," he said. "Start off so you're a bit chilled 'cause you'll warm up as we go."

It was not long before Diver Dan's engine could be heard coming over the mountains again. It landed just as it had on the prior two occasions and Hempstead was delighted to see Elaine emerge from the plane. He had been in charge long enough.

"We're lucky, we got it all in three trips," she said walking up to see that the gear was properly loaded on the sleds. "You guys do good work." She looked over toward Jim as if to acknowledge her inappropriate choice of pronouns.

With their clients idly watching, Hempstead and Elaine prepared the final sled with the remaining contents from the plane. When they were finished, Elaine went to speak with Diver Dan, who was still in the cockpit with the engine running.

"We'll plan to meet you back here at twelve o'clock in the afternoon in exactly three weeks," she said. "If anything changes in our plans, I'll ask a ranger to radio and let you know."

Wishing them all luck, Diver Dan gave them a thumbs up before he swung the plane around and shortly put it back into the air. The departing gesture of humanity made Hempstead glad that he had reserved judgment and not wasted much contempt on him before. And as the plane vanished over the horizon, he thought about it being his last contact with civilization for a long while. He also wondered whether Diver Dan would actually remember the rendezvous time or location in three weeks. But apart from his usual skepticism, there was no good reason to doubt him.

Elaine organized them into a single-file line in the snow. Hempstead was in the front, the Chicago contingent was in the middle, and she was at the end. Each of them was towing a sled full of gear and carrying a sixty-pound pack. When they were ready Hempstead began taking on the glacier at a leisurely slow pace--there was no need to waste energy racing up the glacier. Even at this rate, however, the effects of the altitude were apparent. They were all breathing hard and quickly tired. But other than that, it was simply a long and direct path they were setting. Using two full days to reach Kalhitna Base Camp would give them an opportunity to acclimate.

It was a very gentle grade up the glacier. Every once in a while their progress was slowed by the need to circumnavigate a crevasse. Elaine looked ahead for the dimpled and depressed contours in the snow before them that marked a lurking crevasse disguised by a slight layer of snow. At that relatively easy part of their journey there was no good reason or excuse for falling into one, but it happened all of the time to climbers who had been lulled by the simplicity of the terrain into letting their guard down.

When they finally arrived Camp One was full of people. The weather had been wonderful and accommodating the last several days allowing many groups to summit via the West Buttress and return to the camp prior to repeating the long march back down the glacier.

There was litter and discarded equipment all around them and, without the wind, there was the aroma of an open latrine. Hempstead was amazed that in the middle of nowhere such a place could become so recklessly tarnished by its human inhabitants. Meanwhile, the Chicago contingent had gone off to talk to a group of women climbers who had summited two days earlier leaving Hempstead and Elaine alone to set up camp.

"Hey guys, you want to be a part of this climb?" She yelled over to them. "Why don't you give us a hand over here?"

They were obviously embarrassed and quickly came to help. So much for high altitude romance.

When the tents were erected, they all went into Jim and Elaine's tent where Hempstead had begun to boil water for brewing hot tea. It was an extremely confined space, but with the good weather, Hempstead was able to keep the stove working outside giving them just a little more room.

"We'll leave for Camp Two tomorrow with half our gear," Elaine said while performing some minor repairs on her crampons. "We'll stow it there and come back down to take another load up the next day. Let's try to get plenty of rest tonight because we're gonna leave here as early as we can."

The tent fell silent except for the constant hissing of the small gas stove just outside the entrance. After they ate and drank as much water as they could, they went to sleep in their separate tents. The real climbing was about to begin.

Chapter 11

Keith had an early doctor's appointment. The condition in his mouth was getting worse and he was disturbed that he was being kept waiting in the reception area.

"Mr. Warren, would you please come with me?" The nurse was a heavy-set black woman. She turned and held the door to the hall leading to the examination rooms open for him.

Keith followed her out of the lobby and she pointed him into a small examining room.

"I'm just going to do some routine checks before the doctor sees you," she said as she was putting on her rubber gloves. "Would you please take off your shirt so I can listen to your heart and chest?"

Keith complied and then stood there helplessly as she fumbled about a drawer. She set the items on a cloth-covered tray before turning her attention back to him.

Placing a thermometer in his mouth she said, "Keep this under your tongue for a few minutes." While it was in place, she listened to his heart and made some notes on her clipboard. "Take some deep breaths for me, please." She was now listening to his lungs. She made some more notes before she removed the thermometer and read it. More notes. "I'm going to take some blood now, then the doctor will be in."

"Well, how do I look?"

"Pretty good, although you have a slight temperature." She was swabbing his arm with iodine. "You're going to feel a little sting, but it won't last long." She stuck the needle in this arm and filled two vials with his blood. When she was done, she cleaned his arm and put a Band-Aid on it.

"The doctor will be in shortly." She removed her rubber gloves, discarded them and left the room.

Keith sat on the examining table looking for something to read while he waited. He was a little chilled without his shirt in that sterile environment. Before too long the door swung open.

"Good mooring, Mr. Warren, I'm Dr. Lash." He was already reading the notes that his nurse had made. "What seems to be the problem?" He placed the notes on the counter.

"I've got these white sores all over my mouth," he said, "and it's very difficult to talk." He sat for a moment as Dr. Lash was putting on his rubber gloves. "And they're getting worse."

"Let's have a look." The doctor had a wooden tongue depressor in one hand and a pen light in the other. He stretched Keith's mouth into several unnatural formations. "Hold your tongue out for a moment, please." The examination continued. "Thank you," he said clicking off the pen light.

"What is it, Doctor?"

Dr. Lash didn't answer, but instead stood in front of Keith and felt the glands on his neck. "Lie down, please, and loosen your pants." He felt the glands in Keith's pubic area. "All right, you can get dressed now," he said making his own notes on the clipboard.

"Well, what is it Doctor?" he asked again.

"I'm not sure, and want to see the results from your blood work. You have a thrush-like condition in your mouth, swollen glands and a slightly elevated temperature. Your body is definitely fighting something," he said, "how have you felt, generally?"

"Fine, except for this stuff in my mouth. Can't you just give me something for it?"

"I'm going to write you a prescription that should clear that up. In the meantime, we'll send your blood to the lab. I should have a better picture when I get the results back.

Should be about three days." He handed Keith the prescription he had written out. "Why don't you plan on coming in at the same time on Friday morning."

"Sounds good, Doc." Keith was already dressed and followed the doctor out of the door.

"I'll need to see Mr. Warren on Friday morning at nine o'clock," Dr. Lash said to his office staff.

Keith left and drove to a pharmacy. He had his prescription filled, which was some sort of mouthwash that he was required to use three times each day. As soon as he got back in the car, he took his first dose of the medicine.

Chapter 12

Jim Hempstead kissed her the moment he awoke. "Look where I've ended up," he said.

She stretched, yawned and spoke all at the same time. "Freezing your ass off in a tent on the side of Denali?"

"I'm happy and in love."

"I think the altitude must be getting to you."

"Fuck you," he said and pulled her toward him.

"You want our esteemed clients to hear?"

"Fuck them."

"Nope, just you."

When they came out of their tent, Elaine woke up the people in the other tent while Hempstead began brewing tea again. It was not long before they were ready to begin hauling equipment and supplies up to Camp Two. It was four o'clock in the morning and the remainder of the groups had not yet begun stirring in their tents.

It was a cold morning, but there was no wind and it was very tolerable. The grade was much steeper than it had been on their approach to Base Camp so they could no longer use sleds and each was forced to carry as much as they could in their packs.

The group was tied together by a rope with the clients in the middle again. It was important for them all to move at the same speed so that none of them would get pulled off of their feet casting the entire group down the snowy slope. But they weren't moving well at all together. Ken Shepherd was jerking Mitch Geiger forward because Sonny O'Neil, who was behind Geiger, was having trouble keeping up, which in turn would jerk Geiger backwards when the rope became taut between them. The result was that Geiger was getting jerked forward and then backward, this whipsaw effect being completely out of his control.

"Slow down!" Geiger angrily screamed ahead to Shepherd.

"Try to keep up, Sonny," Elaine yelled up to him. "We have to move as a group and keep a good pace."

Sonny O'Neil was obviously having problems and they were all becoming upset with one another. They weren't two hours out of Kalhitna Base Camp, and still eight thousand feet from the summit when Sonny O'Neil finally dropped to his hands and knees and began violently puking all over discoloring the pristine snow.

"It can be a lot of things," Elaine told the rest of them. "Altitude does funny things to people, doesn't it, Jim?" She gave him her smirk. "He might just need some more time to adjust to it." She put her hand on Sonny O'Neil's shoulder. "Can you make it to Camp Two? We're not the Marines, we don't have to take this mountain."

"Yea, I can make it," he said wiping some slime from his mouth. "Just need to rest a minute."

They left Sonny O'Neil alone with his puke and what was left of his dignity as Elaine corralled Ken Sheperd and Mitch Geiger off to the side.

"Look," she said, "I'm gonna plant him at Camp Two. The rest of us will split up his load. If he doesn't get dramatically better by tomorrow, the climb is off. We're too far from the summit to leave him planted while we go up. We'll have no choice but to go back down. I mean, we haven't even started the real uphill part of this thing yet."

There was an unspoken recognition between them that Elaine's proclamation was the right thing to do, but would likely cost them the summit. Sonny was showing no signs of improvement as they took their time reaching Camp Two. When they finally reached it, there was only one other tent resting on a dug out snow platform. Drooping and awkwardly listing to the side, it had obviously been clumsily thrown together. They set up a tent on a snow platform next to it and placed Sonny in it surrounded by sleeping bags and full water bottles.

"Here, take these," Elaine said handing him some pills.

"What are they?" he asked.

"Diamox. They'll help with the altitude."

When Sonny was secure, the rest of them prepared to head back to base camp and retrieve the rest of their supplies. Outside the occupants of the other tent had emerged and were apparently collecting snow for water.

"Hey dudes," called one of them.

The other did not bother to remove the headphones that were delivering clamorous music directly to his central nervous system. When Hempstead walked over to them he noticed their snowboards propped against the other side of the tent. He could also smell the sweet scent of burnt marijuana about them.

"What's up guys?" He looked quizzically at their boards.

"Workin' our way up," one of them said. "We're gonna shred this mountain."

"From the top?"

"Any other place, Dude?"

"How long you guys gonna stick around?"

"Thought we'd hang for another day or so to acclimate. We're the 'Usual Suspects.' I'm Jeremy," he pointed to his friend, "and that's Andy."

The park service requires all climbers to register the names of each individual in the group. Many teams also opt to register a group name that connotes something about them. Hempstead was not certain what the 'Usual Suspects' insinuated about Jeremy and Andy, but he was pretty well convinced that they were nuts and would likely come off of the mountain in body bags.

"We've got to leave one of our friends in the tent over here while we go back to base camp for supplies," he said. "Can you guys kinda keep an eye on him?"

"Cool," Jeremy answered.

Without Sonny O'Neil, the descent was relatively easy and they were back at camp well before dusk, which was more crowded by the other groups that had arrived throughout the day. They put on warm and dry clothes before gathering together in one tent and starting to brew up tea. Their conversation meandered but basically drifted back to a concern for Sonny and a hope that he would improve.

"Hey, Princessa, I heard you were up here," the man sticking his face in the tent said.

"Jack? Jack Bates, is that you? Well come on in for some tea!" She was obviously happy to see him.

Jack Bates was a tall handsome man blessed to look even ruggedly better after time in the mountains. He had dark tousled hair and a beard that seemed neatly fixed at about four or five days of growth.

Bates had pioneered several routes up Denali, and had many first ascents to his name. Neither Jack Bates nor Elaine offered an explanation for their acquaintance. So Hempstead occupied himself trying to prevent his imagination from getting the best of him.

Elaine handed Bates a cup of hot brew. "I had heard you might be up here, Jack. How's it been this year?" she asked.

"A lot of bad shit on the mountain," he said. "Until now, the weather's been miserable."

"What's been going on?" Ken Shepherd asked.

"I've personally been involved in two rescues, and the rangers can't keep up with the rest. It's been grim, really grim."

"Care to share any of it with us?" Mitch Geiger asked.

"You know, the usual. These Japanese climbers come over here with no training and no guides and try to Kamikaze their way to the top. That usually means Japanese stew all over some crevasse at the bottom of the Orient Express."

"How's your group this time?" Elaine asked.

"Good, they're climbing pretty strong. Not like my last bunch."

111

"These guys are pretty strong, too," she said. "But we had to plant their friend up at Camp Two today."

"I thought I'd seen it all until my last bunch," he laughed. "I had five people, including some guy and his fiancée. We get to Camp Three and this idiot starts telling us about all the shit that he's climbed. I knew right away that it was trouble. It's eight o'clock at night and all of a sudden he tells us he's gonna go out and scale the col for a view. I mean, we told him he was crazy, but, you know, we're just guides, not cops. So he kisses his fiancée and tells her he'll be back shortly, puts on his crampons and leaves the tent." Jack Bates sipped some tea and thought for a moment. "Anyway, about two hours later, we hear this guy screaming for help. By now, its snowing hard and none of us really feels like going out to get him. Phil Davidson was with me, Elaine. He yells up 'Are you hurt?' We wait for a second. 'No,' comes the answer out of the night. 'Wrong answer,' Phil yells back up the mountain. By this time the guy's fiancée is flipping out. She's screaming at us to go retrieve him. Phil is screaming back at her that her fiancée was a dumb shit. Then this pathetic little guy starts screaming at his fiancée to get someone to come help, and she's screaming at us and then Phil's screaming back at her."

The whole tent was erupting with laughter.

"Finally, when the whimpers began to fade, I got dressed and went to find him. He was only about five hundred yards from the camp, but with no headlamp, he was scared shitless to move any further. When I got to him, he was so cold that he had taken off his underwear and put it on his head to help keep him warm. I marched his ass back into the tent, underwear and all. You should'a seen the look on his fiancée's face. Here's the man of her dreams, gonna take care of her for the rest of her life, being paraded around in front of everyone with his underwear on his head. Needless to say, the climb was over for them, and it was a long quiet walk back down the mountain over the next several days.

Don't know whether they ever got married. Guess you could say they had their own special alpine experience."

They sat up late listening to Jack Bates tell stories. Everyone was still laughing about what had become of "underwear man" when he finally got up to leave. The laughter put everyone at ease for the first time since they had begun to climb.

"It's getting late," Jack Bates said as he stood to leave and kissed Elaine on the cheek. "Good to see you up here, Elaine."

"You too, Jack."

After he was gone, Elaine told them that if she were ever in trouble in the mountains, Jack Bates was the guy she'd want coming after her.

"Wonder why people like Jack put their lives on the line for all these first ascents?" Ken Shepherd asked.

Fuck Jack Bates, Hempstead thought.

"Mountains will be here forever," Elaine answered. "Some people think that if you tag your name to a mountain, you live on forever."

"What do you think?" Mitch Geiger asked.

"I think the mountains are a place for quiet achievements and failures."

Before long the lights were out and they all went to sleep quickly, except for Hempstead. The only way he could break his fixation over Jack Bates was to think about his son. So he sat up in his sleeping bag with his head brushing the top of the tent reassuring himself that he had no alternative other than to be where he was.

In time he finally laid down and put his arm around Elaine as she slept. When he did, the bad thoughts all went away and he did not let go of her for the rest of the night.

The next day was sunny and warm. Carrying the rest of their gear to Camp Two, they were climbing strong without Sonny O'Neil in tow. After about four hours of work they arrived and found Sonny rested and feeling much better.

113

There was no sign of the "Usual Suspects" and Hempstead asked him if he'd seen them.

"Are those the guys that were in the next tent?"

"Yea, when'd they leave?"

"Early this morning, before the sun was up. They had their music playing pretty loud last night and Roger came to see what was going on."

"Who's Roger?"

"Said he was a ranger. I told him I wasn't with them and he went to check so I followed him. Those guys were lying in the snow flapping their arms and legs up and down making snow angels. Before Roger could identify himself, they offered us mushrooms and mini-bottles of tequila."

"I knew those guys were crazy," Jim said.

"That's what Roger thought. Told them that they had to leave to get off of the mountain in the morning or he would radio a helicopter and have them lifted out. That was the last that I saw of them. Roger spent the night in here."

Elaine looked at Hempstead and shook her head holding back a laugh. "Tomorrow is a big day," she said. "It's gonna be steep and long. When we get to Camp Three, we'll be within striking distance but it'll be a long way back. I need to know now, honestly, whether each of you is ready to continue."

They all knew her question was directed at Sonny.

"I can do it, guys," he said. "I'm not the lightweight that you think I am."

There was no more discussion, they were going for the top.

Chapter 13

The medicine had worked. Keith's mouth lost any evidence of the white scourge that had taken it over. Drink had been pretty good to him that afternoon and the telephone was ringing as he walked into his empty house.

"Yes, this is Keith Warren."

"Mr. Warren, this is Nancy Slocum from Dr. Lash's office. Your blood work has arrived, and he'd like to make sure that you're still coming in the morning."

"Hey, tell him I'm fine, everything is all cleared up and thanks a lot."

"I think he'd like to talk to you about your blood work anyway."

"Why, is something wrong? Can't you tell me?"

"I'm not qualified to interpret results, but I do know the doctor would like to see you."

"Is nine o'clock still all right?"

"We'll see you then, thanks."

Keith woke early the next morning. He had hardly slept wondering why the doctor had wanted to see him. Probably routine.

He arrived at the doctor's office fifteen minutes early. Instead of making him wait in the reception area, the same nurse took him immediately to a private office instead of an examining room. Dr. Lash was already there sitting in a plush black leather chair and wearing a business suit. He was reading a report and had not yet dawned a lab coat for the day.

"Mr. Warren, I've got your test results," he said when they were alone. "I'd like to run another series of blood work."

"What's going on, Doc?"

115

"Your results show the presence of an antibody that is only present with HIV. These things are not necessarily conclusive, and that's why I want to run a second test."

Keith's body filled with adrenaline and his mind with denial. Nothing had changed in the entire universe in the last thirty seconds except for Keith Warren's life. It had become instantly bifurcated into pre-diagnosis and post-diagnosis perspectives. He looked at the black leather chair and attempted to retreat in his mind to the first time that he had seen it only moments earlier.

"I feel fine, Doctor. I don't know how this could be. It's gotta be a mistake."

"Maybe, but it might explain your low-grade fever, swollen glands and yeast infection," he said. "Let's get another test before we overreact."

"What do I do? I mean, do I just go on as usual until we check this thing out? Can I take something?"

"You should act as if you are infectious. No unprotected sex or exchange of bodily fluids." He handed Keith a pamphlet. "Let's leave it at that until we confirm this one way or another. I'm very sorry to have to tell you this."

Dr. Lash took him to an examining room where the nurse drew his blood again. He stared at the tube with disgust as it turned red with his poisoned fluid. When it was over he walked out of the examination room feeling extremely self-conscious. Everyone most certainly knew of the news he had just received. He did not bother to check with the women at the reception area when he left.

Keith could not go to work. It was not within him to even want a drink or to think about women. He just drove in his car. He changed the radio station in a pitiful search for a song he had never heard. He could not stand to listen to any music that he had known from his previous life. He needed a new song for his new existence. Everything else was irrelevant. He couldn't find one. For the first time in his life, Keith Warren was forced to face the consequences-- indeed the deadly consequences-- of his actions.

Chapter 14

It had snowed all night. The weight of it on their tents made the ceilings sag to inches above their heads. Hempstead swatted the roof with his hand causing the snow to fall away and the tent to rebound into its intended shape. The warm breath coming from their bodies and cast against the cold tent walls had condensed throughout the night making everything outside of their sleeping bags sticky and wet.

Elaine poked her head outside. "Looks like we'll be kicking some steps today," she said turning back to him.

A foot or so of fresh snow had fallen erasing the paths that previous groups had made for them. They were going to have to establish a new trail and whoever led the way up in the deep fresh powder would suffer the arduous task of kicking and packing the snow in an effort to form snowy steps for the others to follow.

"Why don't I start off in the lead and we'll use you as the anchor belay?" Hempstead said. "Besides, the strongest climber should go last." He reached over and affectionately squeezed her bicep.

"You can kick for a while and we'll switch at some point. You wouldn't deny me that pleasure would you?"

Before too long they were all climbing up the mountain again. Hempstead was in the lead followed by the Chicago contingent, and then Elaine. As soon as they began it started snowing again and the visibility became very poor so that each climber had to focus on the feet of the person in front. If they looked up for even a moment, the driving snow would crystallize on their goggles like a car windshield in an ice storm rendering them virtually blind.

Hempstead was working hard to establish a route in the ever-increasing snow cover. The slope was extremely steep and he chose a path that was a series of switchbacks helping ease the effects of the grade, but causing the group to travel in a serpentine-like manner up the mountain face.

Working hard in the lead, Hempstead's mind and body settled into a slow but steady rhythm. Kick, rest, step. Kick, rest, step. Each step felt like he was running a mile at sea level and the resting pauses between steps became longer and longer.

It was cold and yet he was sweating enormously. Hempstead was becoming concerned not only about dehydration, but also about the chill that would come when he stopped exerting himself. Those two concerns created a minor dilemma. If he stopped for water he would become instantly chilled. If he didn't, he would become dehydrated. So Hempstead plodded on and their progress remained slow with the ever-increasing snowfall. The wind gusts came and went stirring up the fresh snow from the ground and giving it a chance to fall in blustery swirls all over again.

He shortly resolved his dissonance. At a place where the slope became somewhat forgiving, he stopped and signaled the others to come join him.

"Let's take some water here," he said. Before he drank he pulled a fleece jacket from his pack and put it on under his parka. He was determined to stay as warm as was possible.

"I wish I could see where we're climbing," Mitch Geiger said. His goggles had frosted over and his blue and frozen face looked as if it could crack apart at any second.

Sonny O'Neil was bent over resting his hands on his thighs in an effort to transfer the weight of his pack momentarily off of his back. "I just wish my fucking legs would stop pounding."

Elaine momentarily left the huddled group and walked a little further up the slope where she kicked a few steps into the fresh powder. She came back and removed a folding

118

shovel from her pack and then walked back to her freshly-kicked steps and started digging in the snow.

"What's she doing?" Sonny O'Neil asked still breathing very hard. He looked miserable as the affects of the altitude began to reemerge with a telling expression all over his face.

"She's checking avalanche conditions," Hempstead told him. "The warm spell we had for a while softened the old snow. Put this new fluffy stuff on top of it and the conditions are right for a giant snow skid. She's digging down and checking the snow layers out to see if we're walking into a potential slide."

Just then it started to blow even harder causing the snow to fall horizontally with the full force of the wind. The ice particles painfully pelted their faces and visibility became nearly zero. At the same time the temperature had dropped dramatically as it can do in an instant above the Arctic Circle. They were in a blizzard.

She came back down to them again. "Grab your shovel, Jim, I don't like the snow," she said. "We're gonna dig a cave and hunker down 'til this passes." She was already at work. "The rest of you keep as warm as you can and cover your faces."

Hempstead was glad to be exerting himself again and generating some heat. They took turns filling their shovels and depositing the snowy contents to the side. They were boring directly into the side of the mountain.

By this time the temperature had dropped to well below zero. There was no telling what it was with the wind chill. The Chicago contingent stood huddled, silent and shivering. They took turns complaining that their toes were becoming numb and their fingers throbbing with pain. It was the price they were forced to pay as the blood left their extremities to protect their internal organs from the cold.

Hempstead and Elaine's teamwork began to pay off. They were both inside the snow cave carving out and enlarging opposite sides of the cavity. When it was just large enough, they called upon their clients to come join

119

them inside. They were amazed at how the snow provided such remarkable insulation from the wind and cold outside.

When they were all situated there was virtually no room for movement. If they were forced to stay there for a while, they would all have to sleep sitting up. Hempstead lit the stove and started brewing up some hot tea. As soon as he did, Sonny O'Neil began puking all over himself again. The stench quickly filled the thin arctic air that was trapped inside.

"Go ahead and fill this up if you need to, Sonny." Hempstead had tunneled further back into the snow to create a make-shift latrine. Each time it was filled, he put fresh snow over the contents.

The snow was quickly accumulating outside the cave and it began blocking the entrance. The new snow helped shield the wind from coming throughout the opening, but they had to keep it from completely closing so they wouldn't lose the ventilation that was protecting them from an excessive, and potentially deadly, carbon dioxide buildup. They were no longer free to exit the cave at will, and were forced to crawl over one another to go to the back of the cave to relieve themselves in Sonny O'Neil's toilet.

"Are we having an alpine experience?" Ken Shepherd joked.

"You got it," Elaine said. "The mountains have many moods and if you're going to climb one, you better like 'em all."

"Yeah, well, the next time you plan our vacation, Mitch, why don't we try for a beach experience?" Ken Shepherd reached over and rubbed Mitch Geiger's head with his fist.

When the contents of his stomach were emptied, Sonny O'Neil could no longer throw up and he began gasping with the dry heaves. Yellow bile was running down the side of his face and dangling from his chin. He looked completely distressed curled up in the corner simply staring at the walls of the cave and holding himself as his body jittered and his teeth chattered.

Just then, there was a tremendously loud crack followed by the sound of rumbling thunder that came from the direction they had been heading toward. The cave began to vibrate wildly. It sounded as if a freight train was coming down upon them.

"Oh shit! Avalanche." Elaine knew it immediately.

They sat helplessly until it all ended as suddenly as it began. It was immediately still and quiet again except for the wind.

"Good call, honey," Hempstead said in a shaken voice. He sat there for a moment and thought about the obvious consequences if they had gone on that day. "We probably just avoided some body surfin' and Ken could have had his beach experience and alpine experience all rolled up in one," Hempstead said disguising that Elaine's judgment had probably just saved all of their lives.

It was getting late and it was still snowing hard. By this time, all but Sonny O'Neil had come to lie against the others for support and warmth. He simply smelled too much like vomit to participate in the bonding. Under the conditions, the best any of them could hope for was intermittent instances of something approaching sleep. The only place worse in the world was outside.

They laid together quietly listening to the sounds of the wind and Sonny O'Neil moaning next to the latrine. Before they tried to sleep, Elaine looked at Hempstead in a manner that clearly signaled the end of their bid for the summit of Denali. They would tell their clients in the morning.

"Tum de dum de dum ... " she spoke softly as she tried to get some rest.

Chapter 15

Keith Warren was not interested in the results of his second blood test. He had resolved that his last visit with Dr. Lash was in fact a confirmed AIDS diagnosis and that he would be kidding himself to hope otherwise. It was two days after he heard the news before he could even emerge from his house. He had not eaten and had slept very little. Instead, he spent most of his time staring blankly at whatever was on the television set. It seemed to him as if there were suddenly more news stories and advertisements about AIDS than he had ever heard before.

When he finally left that night, Keith had decided that he would find a bar where nobody knew him and he could drink alone. He drove downtown--still no new songs on the radio. The neon sign flashed West End Tavern and attracted him to pull over to the curb in front. He was greeted inside by the smell of stale cigarette smoke and cooking grease that lingered in the air because the exhaust fan had not worked for many years.

Keith sat down on the red patent leather bar stool and ordered a Budweiser and a shot of Jack Daniels. He was comforted that nobody was attempting to make conversation with him and he quickly ordered several more rounds.

It was not long before the alcohol began working. He was relaxed and in the process of convincing himself that he would be the first person ever to survive his disease when his beeper silently buzzed in his pocket. He recognized the number as an invitation for passion.

He ordered another beer and another shot before he returned the call and made arrangements for the evening. Keith was feeling much better and was drunkenly oblivious to, or had rationalized away, the risk to which he was about to expose to his unwitting companion. He left the West End Tavern feeling much better about things.

The next morning Keith arrived home devoid of the confidences that the West End Tavern had given him the night before. He was back on the couch watching television when the telephone rang.

"Mr. Warren, this is Dr. Lash." He had not bothered to have a nurse or assistant make this call. "Your results are back and I'd like to see you as soon as you can get here."

"I know, there's no need for me to come in," he said darkly.

"Mr. Warren, there is a lot that we can do and a lot that we need to talk about. Please come and I'll see you whenever you get here."

"Thank you, Doctor."

What little hope that some unrealized portion of Keith's psyche had held out for a miracle was gone: he instantly dropped below the point that he had thought was rock bottom.

Chapter 16

It had stopped snowing sometime during the night. When the clouds cleared there was no longer any insulation from the cold and the temperature plummeted in the arctic night to fifty degrees below zero.

The people inside the snow cave had slept very little and, with the morning sun shining through the ventilation hole in their doorway, they were oblivious to the magnitude of the chill that awaited them outside. Sonny O'Neil was still in his corner quivering from the onset of dehydration brought about by his continued inability to keep anything in his stomach.

Elaine held out a container of water. "You need to drink as much of this as you can, Sonny."

"I don't have the energy to take it from you."

She held a plastic jar to his mouth and carefully poured the water in as fast as Sonny O'Neil could consume it. He did not take very much before he rolled over onto his side and began shaking violently again.

"I've made a decision during the night," she announced to everyone. "Apart from the fact that Sonny isn't going anywhere, with all the new snow, the risk of avalanche is just too great for us to continue with this thing."

There was a long hush within the cave. The tremendous disappointment that Mitch Geiger and Ken Shepherd felt was all over their faces.

"I'm sorry," she continued, "but just as soon as we can get Sonny on his feet, we're going back down. This mountain will still be here whenever you want to try it again."

Hempstead looked up and was momentarily startled to see a face staring back in through the opening in the cave. "What can we do for you, man?" he asked.

"Elaine, is that you in there?" Asked the voice from outside.

"Who wants to know?"

"Goddamit, I'm glad to see you, Elaine."

"Jack?"

"Yeah, its me. It's a tragedy," he said edging his way into their protection. "A terrible tragedy." Jack Bates cleared some more of the entrance allowing the cold air to fill the cave before he realized there was no room for him inside. "I need your help, Elaine." His eyes were pasted open and his face was expressionless. He had obviously been through an ordeal.

She offered him some hot tea. "What's going on, Jack?"

He stood for a moment without saying a word and pretended to sip the tea. "I lost 'em. My clients are up there in an epic cluster fuck of a mess_"

"Jack!" she interrupted. "Tell me what is going on."

"We took a fall, Elaine. I fucked up. We unroped to take a break. That avalanche hit and everyone jumped in different directions sending us down. I don't know how long they can last. I don't even....."

She interrupted him again. "Where are they Jack, what is their condition?" She was already getting her gear together and checking her pack for supplies. "Are any of them able to move under their own power?"

"They're at least a thousand feet up. I don't know, Elaine, they've been bivouacked all night. Can't think any of 'em could have taken it."

It wasn't like Jack Bates to be this disoriented. It was clear to her that he didn't know the condition of his clients and was himself in some level of shock. It would be useless to press him for more information. "Can you take me up?"

He just shook his head.

"Jim, I want you to wait here," she said. "You've got plenty of food and it's safe."

"I can help, Elaine. These guys will be all right here."

"No, Jim. Stay here with them."

It was no more than fifteen minutes after Jack Bates had arrived than he was roped up to Elaine and hiking up in the direction that she was hopeful would take them to his clients.

She stopped them for a moment and turned back toward the cave. Hempstead was staring plaintively up toward her.

"If I'm not back by morning," she called, "you can start taking them down if the weather looks good."

He didn't respond. It was not within his being to accept any possibility that Elaine might never return to him. He just blew her a kiss.

Chapter 17

Keith arrived at Dr. Lash's office just minutes before his nine o'clock appointment. He pretended to read a magazine to avoid making eye contact with anyone. They didn't keep him waiting there very long.

"Dr. Lash will see you now." It was the same nurse that had escorted him to the doctor's office the last time and she showed him there again.

"Please get the door on your way out," the doctor said to her once Keith was situated in his chair. When she was gone he looked Keith squarely in the eyes and said "your first test has been confirmed, Mr. Warren."

Keith showed and felt no emotion--it had all left him over the course of the last week.

Dr. Lash continued. "You're probably in the very early stages of this thing. You've not developed full-blown AIDS and there are a great number of new treatments. I'd like to refer you to a specialist and a psychiatrist."

"Sure, Doctor, give me their names."

"Mr. Warren, a great many people have been diagnosed with this disease and are living extraordinarily normal lives. This is not the short-term death sentence that it was just five years ago." He went on to explain in detail an "AIDS Cocktail" that combined "older generation" drugs such as AZT and 3TC with newer protease inhibitors such as saquinavir or ritonavir that, while expensive, significantly eliminated the symptoms although did not wipe out the virus.

He wasn't listening at all. "I know, Doctor," he said when the words had stopped.

"I want you to start thinking about something that is extremely important. I don't know, or care, whether you're gay, straight, or something else. But anyone that you might

127

have given this to should know as soon as possible that they should be tested."

Keith nodded his head and stared at his hands folded in his lap. He almost chuckled at the irony of his wife being the only woman that he knew that was probably not at risk.

"Thank you, Doctor, I appreciate your help." He took the cards with the names of the referrals and left the office.

Until that moment, Keith had not even thought about where he had gotten the disease or to whom he might have transmitted it. He didn't care about most of the women he had been with. The only person that he was concerned at all about was Diane O'Rourke. He was not certain, however, whether he had the courage to tell her.

Chapter 18

Not even all of their effort to quickly reach Jack Bates' clients could protect them from the effects of the bitter cold. Elaine's fingers were becoming numb and she could feel the stinging in her toes. The perspiration on the exposed portions of her hair froze causing icicles to form and dangle from underneath her hat.

Unable to locate the tracks from Bates' descent the night before, they were kicking steps in the heavy new snow. And although they were moving quickly without clients, Elaine sensed that Jack Bates was having trouble. After all, he had been awake and struggling in this environment for over twenty-four hours.

He stopped briefly for water and looked up surveying the terrain. "My best guess is we gotta go about five hundred more feet in this direction," he said pointing up roughly in the same direction they had been climbing.

Soon after they started again the route became so steep that their bodies were nearly lying against the snowy and nearly vertical slope and they were forced to climb as if there was an invisible ladder between them. Their simple movements were becoming difficult to execute. Bates would reach as high above him as possible and sink his ice ax into the snow for support. When it was secure, he would raise his left foot as high as it would go and drive the front points of his crampons into the snow. With his left foot anchored, he would use it as a step to bring his right foot up to the same position. He repeated the exhausting process up the face. Elaine did the same twenty feet behind him and if either of them fell, there was little hope that the other would be able stop them both from embarking upon a fatal tumble down the mountain.

It had been several hours since they stopped for water before they came to a rise where the angle of the slope eased somewhat. They were breathing hard and decided to rest.

After only a moment Elaine spotted a small and bright red lump in the snow. It was lying at the base of another steep, but shorter, incline.

"What's that?" She pointed to it and unclipped herself from the rope to go for a look.

She walked for about fifteen yards before picking the mitten up from the snow and holding it high for Jack Bates to see. His head dropped in immediate recognition.

"That's Donna's," he said when she brought it back to him.

"We must be close, Jack. Let's keep moving." Elaine clipped herself back onto the rope.

They walked over toward the incline where she had found Donna's glove. It did not take long for them to reach the crest and another plateau.

"Mother fuck," Jack Bates said reaching the top.

Elaine came up to meet him. "Jesus," she whispered to herself and unclipped from the rope again. "Who is it, Jack?"

"It's Donna."

Donna was sitting upright in the snow with her knees brought up to her chest and her arms wrapped around them. She was missing a glove and her exposed hand was an unnatural gray color. Their arrival produced absolutely no expression at all from her.

He put his face down directly in front of hers. "Donna, its me, Jack," he said.

She just sat there in her zombie-like state. Her eyes were pasted open and continued showing no emotion. Elaine felt her hand, which was frozen as hard as a rock. She would surely lose it to frostbite, even assuming that they could get her out of this place.

"You are one remarkable woman." Elaine did her best to comfort her and offer encouragement. "We're gonna get you down," she said. "Do you hear me, Donna?"

There was still no response. In a futile gesture Elaine put the missing mitten back on her exposed hand.

"We gotta boil some hot water for her, Jack."

"The others have to be close by," he said.

"I know, but let's get her as warm and safe as possible before we go looking."

The first sip of hot tea was a shock to her body and Donna spit it out. Elaine had wrapped her in a sleeping bag and worked patiently with her to eventually take and hold the tea.

When Donna was fairly well situated, Elaine said, "Why don't you stay here with her and I'll go look around."

Jack Bates just nodded his head again not wasting his energy on words. It was becoming very clear that he was also fast approaching his physical limit.

Elaine removed her binoculars from her pack and searched above for signs of Bates' other two clients. Nothing. She walked about forty more yards and came upon a gaping crevasse. The eerie blue ice formations below were the size of some buildings in large cities. Anything that fell into this crevasse would most likely never found.

She walked along the edge of the abyss looking for signs of where the missing climbers might have fallen in. Another fifty feet from where she first happened upon the crevasse she saw an ice ledge about thirty feet below. On top of the ledge was the grotesque entanglement of two bodies.

She hurried back toward where she had left Jack Bates and Donna. When she was just about upon them she called and asked Bates to come join her.

He immediately got up and headed over to her. "What did you find?" he asked.

"I think I found your other two clients. They took a big fall and are lying in a crevasse over there."

"Are they alive."

"It doesn't look like it, but I'll need a belay down to check it out."

"What'll we do with Donna?"

131

"She's as warm as we can get her. It won't take long to climb down and see what the story is. My guess is that it'll just be the three of us heading back."

They walked back to Donna. Elaine knelt down in front of her face. "We are going to see if we can find your friends," she said. "We won't be gone long. Don't go anywhere, do you understand?"

Donna's eyes expressed understanding before she looked down again at the warm tea that she held in her good hand.

Bates and Elaine made their way back to the edge of the crevasse.

"I'll go down and you belay," she said searching her pack for devices to sink into the snow and create a series of anchors through which to rig the rope pulley system for lowering her into the hole. When she had all the other gear together, she asked Bates to hand her his ice ax.

Bates looked down onto the ledge. "There's no way they made it."

"We gotta check. Ready?"

Bates wrapped the rope around his waist after it came up through the metal anchor dug into the snow. "On belay," he called to her.

Elaine backed her way down off of the lip of the crevasse digging the front points of her crampons into the ice face to ease her weight off of the rope. As she descended, Bates let out just enough rope to allow her to move but kept her fixed in the event of a fall.

Her movements were tentative -she had never seen a dead body before and needed some time to get used to it. There was barely enough room on the ledge for the three of them and she carefully rolled the bodies apart with her feet.

"Ahh!" one of them let out a loud scream that sent Elaine's heart racing with fright.

She looked down and saw the fractured bone that had pierced the woman's clothing and was protruding into the air. Her thigh was shattered in two and the freezing temperatures probably kept her from bleeding to death.

"Can you hear me? What is your name?"

"Oh, God, just let me die."

"I'm Elaine, what is your name?"

"Amy ... Amy Coleman. Ahh ... ."

"Okay, Amy, we're gonna get you outta here." Elaine assessed the other body. Her vital signs barely existed, and there was blood coming from the corner of her mouth. She remained unconscious and there was no way to determine the extent of her internal injuries. "What's your friend's name?"

"Is she dead?"

"No, what's her name?"

"Maddie Weaver." She turned her head to the side and rolled her eyes up into their sockets. "I'm so cold."

"What color is your pain?" Elaine asked. "Tell me the color of your pain."

"I don't know ... oh God ... ."

"Think about your pain, what color is it?"

"It's blue."

"What shape is it?"

"It's a circle, I guess. It's a blue circle."

"I want you to keep thinking about how you're feeling," she said. "Turn your pain a little white dot, okay? Make it the smallest white dot that you can."

Elaine got a pocket knife out of her pack and began cutting lengths of cloth from an extra pair of long underwear. When she was finished she cut the fabric away from around Amy's wound. After exposing the leg she struggled to hold-off the sickness that was building up in her stomach. Fragments of bone, muscle, and torn flesh made a complicated puzzle out of what was once Amy's leg. Elaine knew that she had to act quickly with the flesh exposed to the cold.

"Bite down hard on this," Elaine said putting her wool cap in Amy's mouth.

"AHHG!" Amy passed out from the pain when Elaine suddenly jerked the broken bones of her leg back into place.

She quickly wrapped Amy's cut clothing as much as was possible around the exposed leg. After placing an ice ax like a splint next to the fracture, one by one she tied the shrouds of cloth around the leg securing the ax in place. She then took what was left of the cut-up underwear and wrapped it around the wound to provide further support and protection from the cold.

Perched on the snowy ledge, Elaine unclipped herself from the rope and yelled up to Bates as loudly as she could for more rope. He took a large coil of the rope and threw it down to her. Taking one of the ends, she wrapped it under Amy's arms forming a rope harness which she secured back onto the main line of the rope. When she was finished, she clipped herself back into the rope five feet above where Amy's harness had been secured.

"Climbing!" she yelled back up to Jack Bates.

"Climb on, Elaine."

She began climbing up the ice face with Amy Coleman in tow and still unconscious. The extra weight was a tremendous burden. She was forced to stop and rest after every couple of steps. At that pace it took her over a half of an hour to crest the lip of the crevasse.

"Her leg's broken and she's shocky," she told Bates when she finally got there.

"What about Maddie?" he asked.

Elaine was already unclipping the rope from Amy and preparing for her descent back down. "She's barely alive," she said. "Probably got some internal trauma and she's unconscious. Getting her outta there may do her more harm than good, but I don't think we have a choice."

"Let's do it."

Elaine rappelled back down to the ledge. When she got there, Maddie's eyes were open and fixed, but her body still produced marginal vital signs. She rigged up a rope harness and began working her way back up with Maddie. The ascent required a tremendous effort. She climbed cautiously and it took her twice as long to arrive with Maddie as it did with Amy, rendering her utterly exhausted when she finally reached the top of the crevasse again.

"She's comatose," Bates told her.

"No shit," Elaine said struggling for her breath.

The sun had begun casting ominous orange hues that signaled the approaching night. The sweat that Elaine had generated removing Maddie and Amy from the crevasse was quickly bringing on a clammy chill as it cooled in the twilight air.

"We gotta prioritize, Jack." Elaine heard her voice but it was not her speaking. It all seemed inhumanly distant to her --she was an actor in a play watching herself perform.

"We can keep Donna warm where she is," he said. "We have a better shot with Amy."

"I agree." Elaine understood that their decision meant almost certain death for Maddie.

Jack Bates busied himself with carving out a makeshift snow cave for Maddie and Donna. Amy laid in a sleeping bag with her teeth chattering as Elaine secured a rope to her. A ten foot section trailed from the foot of the bag while the remainder of the rope was fixed so that the upper half of Amy's body could be controlled with it.

With Elaine leading the way and controlling the rope coming from Amy's feet, they began their descent. Bates' job, stationed in the rear, was to keep the rope tight between them and keep Amy Coleman from sliding down the mountain. It was an extremely slow process with Amy writhing in agonizing pain at even the slightest jolt to her shattered leg. Shortly after their departure, it began snowing again.

Back at the snow cave, Jim Hempstead could not chase the demons from his mind. Elaine had left with Jack Bates over six hours ago and, sitting helplessly waiting, he struggled to prevent his thoughts from spiraling hopelessly into a vortex of self-flagellation for abandoning his family. But it was a useless effort. He was a bad father, a bad husband, and he deserved this bad situation. His only solace had been that he had left it all to have Elaine in his life. It had all been justified but now she was somewhere high in the snow on Denali and he could not bear to think about that either.

She was not there to pull him back this time. Sitting helplessly in that over-crowded space that reeked of days of human inhabitancy he could not help but sense that he was finally about to lose everything. He questioned over and over again the decision that had landed him in that place but every concentrated path he took inevitably lead him back to where he was. He was condemned to his snow-cave hell and had been his entire life.

"Tum de fucking dum," he muttered to himself. "Tum de fucking dum."

****

Up high the snow and wind had combined to create white-out conditions. Elaine and Jack Bates spoke very little as they proceeded like drones down the steep mountain face. Elaine would descend just far enough that the rope tethered to Amy became taut. She would then fix herself to the side of the mountain to hold the team secure and await Bates' arrival. The process of lowering Amy down the mountain was slow and, for Elaine and Bates, the intervals without exertion exacerbated the cold. Amy Coleman's journey consisted of sporadic periods of lucidity culminating in pain that sent her back into unconsciousness.

As the darkness came, so did Elaine's thirst. Her mouth was dry and sticky signaling that she had already begun to dehydrate. They came to a nearly vertical slope and stopped. Elaine removed her pack and drank from her water bottle before offering some to Bates. While he was drinking Elaine turned on her headlamp and secured it around her head.

"I think we have enough rope, Jack," she said. "You belay me down this pitch then send Amy to me."

"I've lost a crampon, Elaine." Jack Bates' calmly delivered statement did not mask the announcement of a crisis situation.

That type of perfidy kills people in the mountains all of the time. It was an inexcusable situation. Having just one set of steel points to thrust into the mountain for security, Jack Bates, and thus Elaine and Amy, were severely handicapped and at an increased risk of plummeting down the face of the mountain. Indeed, they were all tied by a rope to a singular fate.

"When did you lose it?" She remained calm knowing that it would do no good to dwell on his negligence.

136

"A while back, it broke in half and slipped right off my boot. Didn't really matter up there but it's gonna make this steeper stuff a little dicey."

Bates was suffering the obvious affects of over-fatigue. He had the blank stare of a person whose brain functions had been reduced to a core and primitive survival mode not unlike a soldier who had seen too much battle.

"Jack, listen to me," Elaine said grabbing his shoulders and staring into those vacant eyes. "I need you to stay with me. Can you hang on until we get back to Jim?"

He nodded his head.

"We're gonna switch. I'll belay you down and you take all the time you need to secure yourself, you hear me? When you're ready, I'll lower Amy to you."

He acknowledged this plan by removing himself from the end of the rope and offering it to her. When Elaine had fastened herself in, he began walking backwards down the face. He was forced to improvise a technique for use with only one crampon using the steel points of his good foot for security. Once his foot position was established, he sunk the point of the ice ax that was in his opposite hand into the snow as low to his body as he could. Holding on, he removed the points of his crampon from the wall and lowered himself until he was again as low as he could go before kicking the points of the crampon back into the wall.

Jack Bates made slow progress. Each time he repeated his routine the rope would jerk Elaine above sending electric-like adrenaline shocks through her body. He eventually made it to the bottom of the wall. His descent required much more effort than a routine one with two good crampons--an effort that was wasting Jack Bates to the point where he was now simply another person to be rescued.

"Off belay," he tried to yell over the wind.

Elaine was not certain what he had said, but assumed from the slack in the rope that he had safely arrived. She pulled the rope up and fixed Amy, who was passed out again, to the end. Elaine carefully lowered Amy down to Bates leaving herself poised alone on top of the snowy ledge. Under normal circumstances, Elaine would have had Bates belay her from his position below. But given his condition, she thought it would be a useless and time-consuming effort. Facing directly against the face of the mountain, Elaine climbed unaided down to Bates and Amy.

"We gotta keep moving," she said. "It's pretty much a walk from here. I'll stay in back to belay, you take the lead. Listen for my voice, Jack. I'll do my best to call out directions."

The group headed down in the snow with Jack Bates aimlessly leading the way and Elaine screaming out directions to him. She was forced to dive into self-arrest countless times to catch the group and it was wearing her down.

The wind and snow diminished as their elevation decreased. They had literally climbed down out of the storm when Bates dropped to his hands and knees and tried to puke up things that were not in his stomach.

"Jack, you gotta hang," Elaine yelled. "Thirty minutes and we're there."

"What's going on?" Amy was momentarily awake and acting hysterically frightened.

"Just stay calm, Amy, we're taking you to the rest of our group."

Bates struggled to his feet and began his way back down the mountain.

"What's going on?" Amy shouted again.

"Just fucking lay calm! We're almost there so go back to sleep." Elaine reached deep down to muster up her patience and her strength. "Look, you're doin' great. Give us a little more time, all right?"

The fresh snow was ankle-high and began balling up in Elaine's crampons. After each step she had to raise the foot that was not supporting her weight and knock out the snow with her ice ax. If she failed to do so, the metal spikes would quickly be turned into skis.

After another hour, the slope eventually eased and walking was not as difficult. Elaine sporadically called out directions to Bates as they meandered closer to the snow cave containing Hempstead and the others.

"Stop for a minute, Jack, we're really close." Elaine cast her headlamp against a snow bank that existed at the top of the steep couloir they were approaching. "There it is." She spotted the cluster of small fluorescent orange flags that Hempstead had stuck into the snow to mark the cave's location.

Jack Bates dropped again to his knees and then lay back in the snow--he had nothing left. Elaine went to the entrance and found the occupants asleep.

"Jim," she was shaking him awake.

"My God, Elaine ... "

"We've got a situation. Boil some water and get these guys up. We need to make this cave a little bigger."

"What's ... "

"I'll tell you later. Right now, Jack and one of his clients need hot tea, warmth, and rest. There are two more up there, Jim."

"Can they make it 'till morning?"

"I don't know, it's snowing pretty hard up high. Look, I'm going back up..."

"Dammit, no you're not. This is not your problem."

"Jim, I'm going back up. Now listen. By the time you get these guys settled it'll be light. I need you to go down and find a ranger. Let him know where the cave is and that we've got one with a compound fracture, one with frostbite, and one with unknown internal injuries."

Elaine changed her clothes, drank some tea, and kissed Hempstead on the lips before leaving again into the night. Only by devoting all of his attention to caring for Jack Bates and Amy Coleman could he keep the demons from creeping back and consuming his thoughts.

Although she was climbing uphill, Elaine's progress was much easier without Bates and Amy. She followed the tracks they had recently left coming down, which prevented her from having to kick new steps into the snow. She eventually came to the headwall that would take her back up into the snow storm. Pausing to check that her crampons were secure and to drink some water, she began to shiver from the chill. She needed to keep moving and focused.

Using two ice axes and the points of her crampons, Elaine worked her way up the wall and into the storm. Her headlamp was of little use so she turned it off and climbed trusting that the section ahead of her was like the section she had just climbed.

Hempstead had settled Jack Bates and Amy into the cave and made them as comfortable as possible. Bates was asleep and Amy was lying quietly whimpering with pain.

Putting on his gloves and crampons, Hempstead turned to his clients, "don't anyone leave until I get back. I'm going to find a ranger."

He walked out of the cave somewhat relieved to be anywhere else and to have a mission that would keep his mind from imagining every step of Elaine's journey. He thought about how the peaceful calm and beauty of the sun rising in the stillness of the morning stood in stark contrast to the tragic plight of the human beings trying to momentarily share this space with the mountain. And for just an instant, he wondered what was happening at that moment in Ohio with the people who were ignorant of his predicament.

Much higher, Elaine had worked her way to the top of the headwall and had begun crossing a steep traverse that led to the crevasse where they had found Amy and Maddie. The snow pounded her and glazed over her goggles. Each of her steps was cautiously placed until she reached the other side of the traverse and the plateau where they had left Donna and Maddie planted in the snow many hours before.

Elaine checked Maddie first. There was no pulse and the life was gone from her eyes. The fall and bivouac had been fatal to her. Donna was alive but extremely hypothermic. She bore the tell-tale gray patches that signaled frostbite all over her face.

"We're getting out of here, Donna. I need you to remain calm."

Donna looked over at the body that had belonged to Maddie.

"She's dead," Elaine told her, "and we need to leave her here. Can you stand?"

Donna struggled to her feet. The tears that came to her eyes began to freeze. Elaine short-roped the two of them together before turning around so that her back faced Donna.

"Climb on my back." Elaine allowed Donna's legs to rest in the creases of her elbows. Slumping forward, Elaine headed back down the plateau toward the traverse and headwall with Donna fixed to her back.

When they arrived at the traverse, Elaine let Donna back down into the snow before working her way across the steep slope putting anchors deep into the snow to serve as protection. She came back to Donna and fixed the rope to her harness and checked her crampons before crossing the traverse again. This time Elaine ran the rope through carabiners attached to the anchors that she had set on the previous trip. If Donna fell, it would only be the distance from one protection point to another.

When Elaine was securely stationed on the other side, she called out to Donna. "Take your time and come to me. Just take your time and come to me."

Donna approached the traverse and then backed off and stood still. Elaine gave her time to think. She tried again, and this time went far enough out onto the face to commit herself to the effort. Her progress was slow and Elaine reeled in the rope as she came to the first carabiner, where she stopped and stood frozen against the wall with her legs shaking.

Elaine shouted to her. "You need to unhook yourself from the rope and place it on the other side of the carabiner."

The frostbite had left Donna with only one working hand, which she used to wildly fumble with the steel devices. Her effort produced a metallic chattering in a dawn that was otherwise devoid of sound. Having developed some odd sort of routine, Donna became better at each anchor point and eventually reached Elaine. The snow was easing so they took some time for water.

Elaine then began fixing the rope to rappel Donna over the headwall. "I'm going to lower you down this wall. Just stay relaxed and when you get to the bottom, don't move."

"What'll we do with Maddie?"

"Maddie is dead. There is nothing we can do for her. Are you ready?"

She nodded her head once and began hesitatingly walking backwards over ledge. Elaine kept the rope tight and only released it as necessary to allow Donna to descend. Donna was barely able to assist with her legs to provide some measure of control so it took an enormous effort for Elaine to lower her. When Donna was down, Elaine cast the rope to her before beginning her own unaided descent.

"We're there," Elaine huffed at the bottom. "It's just a long walk in the snow to Jack and Amy."

They slowly plodded down the mountain short-roped together descending back out of the storm. Every fifteen minutes or so, Elaine stopped to rest. Over sixteen hours after Jack Bates had first reached the snow cave, Elaine arrived again with the last of his remaining live clients.

By that time it was sunny and comparably warm. The Chicago contingent hovered without purpose outside the cave obviously replenished and desiring to get the hell out of there. Jack Bates was awake inside the cave sitting in a sleeping bag and drinking tea, while Amy Coleman had slipped back into unconsciousness.

"I've got Donna here, Jack. A little frostbite, but she'll be all right."

Jack Bates was obviously surprised to see her. "Maddie?"

Elaine looked down and shook her head.

Chapter 19

Like he had done so many other times, Keith Warren picked up the telephone to call Diane O'Rourke and then put it down. Each time, however, he convinced himself that it would be better if he called at a different time during the day. Maybe it was too early ... maybe it was too late ... maybe she was eating ... maybe Joe would answer the phone. His rationalization and procrastination eventually led him to a plan: he would ask her to lunch and tell her face to face the next day. With a course of action firmly in place, Keith spent the rest of the day drinking scotch and watching television having successfully postponed a confrontation until another day.

Chapter 20

Jim Hempstead was singularly focused on his mission, and had purged all other thoughts from his mind. After clearing the headwall below the snow cave, he scampered quickly down the glacier toward Camp Two. Every so often he lost his footing and fell to his knees or his ass, but he would promptly right himself so as not to lose any momentum. On one of those occasions, the points of his crampons punctured his calf muscle, but he felt no pain. It was mid-afternoon and the sun cast warm rays that reflected up from the snow and burned his skin. His glacier glasses kept fogging over from his heat and only when his vision became totally obscured would he stop to wipe them clean.

He was about fifteen hundred feet lower on the mountain than the snow cave when he saw a climber approaching from below. Hempstead put the glasses back on his face and continued his fast-paced descent. The climber had stopped when he saw Hempstead coming down alone and rested awaiting his arrival.

"You haven't seen two guys out here with snowboards have you?" the man asked when Hempstead finally reached him.

He tried to catch his breath before he spoke. "Not lately. I've got some injured climbers up there. I need to find a ranger or a radio."

"Guess it's your lucky day," he said, "I'm a ranger with a radio. My name's Roger. What's up?" he asked calmly.

"Not exactly sure, my partner spent most of the last day pulling people down from up high." He was still catching his breath. "We've got five up there in a snow cave, one with a broken leg and one with some pretty bad internal stuff. We need a helicopter."

"I need to know exactly where they are. I don't know how long it's gonna take to get someone up there, especially with the weather."

Hempstead described their location as best he could while they climbed up higher to a plateau where the direct-line radio worked a little better. Roger was eventually successful radioing for emergency air support but it was getting dark and it would be a problem for the helicopter to locate the cave in the night. They had no assurance when the help might arrive. As soon as they started up the mountain, Hempstead began feeling the pain in his punctured calf and the dread coming on.

****

The only sounds back at the snow cave were the constant hissing of the gas stove melting the snow for the much-needed water supply and the intermittent groans coming from Amy Coleman.

Jack Bates was feeling better and had spread out Elaine's sleeping bag before her. "Get some sleep," he said pointing to the bag.

"I'm too wired," she said. "I just need to sit here and warm up."

"He'll be all right."

"He's not used to climbing alone. This is a big mountain."

"He'll be all right. Get some rest."

But she couldn't sleep, not with Hempstead wandering around alone on the highest mountain in North America. She sat with her back against the snowy wall and her knees pulled up to her chest, and warmed her hands with hot cups of tea.

There were suddenly new voices and sounds coming from outside.

"Hey, anyone home?" called one of them.

"Knock, knock," from another.

Elaine looked up. It was Jeremy and Andy.

Andy peered in the doorway and saw Amy Coleman in her pain. "Looks like something got pretty gnarly around here," he said.

Elaine crawled out of the cave to join them. She sat with them in the calm night outside of the cave happy to have new people involved in her nightmare--people who she didn't have to care for. She listened as they seriously plotted their next climb: the Salathe Wall on acid.

"We didn't need any chemicals to fuck this trip up," she told them.

They looked at her.

"Pretty grim around here, really grim," she said. "It was really blowing hard up there last night. Had to leave a body to get these other two down, it was fairly epic."

"You ok?" Andy asked her.

"Yeah. Had to send my partner down looking for a ranger; he's the one I'm worried about."

"I feel good karma," Jeremy told her.

"Thanks," she said laughing. "We need all we can get around here."

Their vigil lasted until after midnight when they finally heard the mechanical sound of a helicopter off in the distance. They knew then that Hempstead had accomplished his goal.

"I told you, man!" screamed Jeremy. "I told you things felt good around here."

It was a high altitude Lama helicopter that had come all the way from Talkeetna. Its sound intermittently became louder and then softer before it faded and then repeated the pattern. It was searching.

Jumping up and down, Jeremy and Andy began frantically flashing their flashlights and headlamps. Elaine almost laughed at the odd dance of lights they were performing. Almost, until thoughts of Hempstead's safety, which had momentarily been diverted by their antics, came rushing back with a vengeance.

146

"Over here, dude!" Andy yelled as if the pilot could actually hear his plea over the noise of the engine.

The sound became louder again and they could see its lights for the first time. The helicopter had clearly fixed its course on their lights.

It was eventually able to land on the level snow outside the cave. In addition to the pilot, there were two rescue personnel on board. The crew quickly assessed the situation and loaded Donna and Amy on board without stopping the motion of the rotary blades.

Jack Bates hugged Elaine. "Thanks, I owe you big time." He started to climb on board to catch his first ride ever off of a mountain and then turned back to Elaine. "Don't worry, he'll be all right."

The helicopter lifted off throwing snow all about. Soon it was out of sight and before it fell quiet again, Jeremy and Andy were packed and ready to go.

"We're outta here." Jeremy waived at her.

"Guys, it's the middle of the night. Stay until morning," she said. "I don't think I can take any more tragedies and I know I don't have it in me to come after you."

"Yeah, well, probably best if we didn't run into any rangers right now," Jeremy told her. "Later!"

She watched the lights from their headlamps until they disappeared. When she got back in the cave, her clients were all sleeping so she returned to her position with her back against the wall as she sat up waiting for Hempstead. The cave felt a lot emptier and she felt very lonely.

It was still dark out when Hempstead and Roger finally arrived.

"Elaine!" he yelled from outside the cave.

She rushed out to meet him. "God, I was scared for you." She pulled him tight against her. The intensity of her eyes was magnified by her tears. She did not let him go to wipe them away.

He struggled without success for something to say that could adequately express how he felt. All that was available to him in the world was in his arms and he held her tightly.

Neither of them had any energy left. They collapsed together in a mound of abandoned sleeping bags and tried to get some rest. After briefly warming himself, Roger quietly departed in continued pursuit of the 'Usual Suspects.'

Before he drifted into sleep, Hempstead put his arm around her. "Just promise me we'll never do anything again that puts me at any risk of losing you," he said.

"Tum de dum de dum ... "

Chapter 21

"Do you have a minute? May I come in and see you?" He was nervously twisting the coils of the telephone cord.

It had been months since Keith Warren had spoken with Diane O'Rourke. Silence had been the foundation of the awkward detente they had achieved.

Diane let the question pend momentarily before her hesitant voice spoke, "I guess, if you have to."

"Dammit, Diane, don't do me any favors."

"Then maybe it's better if you just speak to me over the phone."

"I need to talk to you, and I can't do it in the office."

"You know where we stand, Keith. I don't know what there is to talk about."

"Will you go to lunch with me today? Don't make me do this over the telephone."

"I'm not going to lunch with you."

Her abject indifference toward him was going to make this easier than he had expected. "Look, it took two, you know. Why are you treating me this way?"

"What do you want Keith?" Her voice grew more impatient.

"I want you to get the hell out of this office so I can privately talk to you about something very important."

"Been there."

That was it. He had given it his best effort but could no longer control his rage. "You and you're fucking husband better go get checked for AIDS." He slammed down the phone.

His phone instantly began ringing. He let it ring. There was little use for him to answer it or to stay at the office. He turned off his computer and walked out his door. As he walked down the crowded hallway, Diane was coming toward him. There was panic all over her face. He tried to step by her, but she grabbed his arm. He jerked it away and kept moving.

"Keith!" she screamed further drawing everyone's attention to them.

He pushed the elevator button and was relieved that it did not take long for one to arrive. He got on and watched as the doors closed in front of him shutting off the mayhem he had just created on the twenty-first floor of his office building.

He wasn't even to his car when his pager began buzzing in his pocket. It was her number and he ignored it. As he pulled out of the parking garage, his car phone was producing the shrill and annoying sounds belonging only to cellular telephones when they ring. He turned it off.

Keith was on his way to the West End Tavern to drink and to be left alone. It wasn't even noon, and the bar was occupied by the same people that were always there no matter when he sporadically showed up in search of anonymity. He took his place on the usual red leather stool and ordered a shot of Jack Daniels and a Budweiser. His pager buzzed and he turned that off too. He threw the whiskey back against his throat and his body instantly quivered in the recognition that it had to begin processing alcohol again.

Several more beers and shots calmed him down and brought him back to a place where he thought he was in control. He wrestled with whether he should ever speak to Diane again or punish her with reciprocal indifference. He achieved what he considered to be a profound intellectual compromise. He resolved that he would reinstate his communication devices and if she contacted him, that would be fine. And if not, that would be fine as well.

Keith paid his bill and walked outside. He was momentarily surprised that it was still daylight. For as drunk as he was, it should have been dark, but he had accomplished a lot in very little time. The top was down on the BMW and the sobering wind felt good against his face. He reached down and turned his phone on. It was ringing.

"Hello."

"Keith, I can't take this." Her voice was scared. "Where can I meet you?"

"I thought ... " he reluctantly declined an opportunity to play games with her. "Meet me at the bar at the Metropolitan Grill."

"When?"

"Now." He hung up the phone.

Keith arrived first and took a seat in the corner of the lounge area. The waiters were busy getting the restaurant ready for dinner service. He finally caught someone's attention and ordered a bottle of Chardonnay. It was open and chilling when Diane arrived.

She sat and looked around as if to see if anyone knew her. Keith tried to fill her glass but she shoved her hand over the top.

"How can you drink?" she asked in consternation.

"Practice."

"How can you act this way?" Her eyes were looking directly at him and pleading with him.

"Look, Diane, you called me. Leave if you want, but I don't need your shit."

"I'm sorry, but you just can't deliver news like this_"

"I tried to get you away, remember?" he interrupted.

"Would you tell me what's going on?" she hushed her voice and looked around again.

Keith took a drink from his glass and then studied its remaining contents for several moments. "I have been diagnosed with the HIV virus. I don't have full-blown AIDS. I don't know where I got this thing, but I thought you should know." He finished the glass of wine and poured himself another.

"You told me the stories_"

151

"Don't start blaming, Diane. It's too late for blame," he interrupted again. "Chances are this means nothing to you. There is very little risk that I could have given this to you, but I wanted you to know and to protect yourself."

She began sobbing and Keith reached for her hand that was resting on the table. She brushed him aside.

"I knew I'd be punished."

"AIDS is not a punishment. It's a very controllable disease these days, and you probably don't even have it."

"How can I tell Joe? Just when things were going so well."

"I wouldn't tell Joe anything unless you have to, Diane. You probably don't have this." He finished his glass and poured himself another.

When the waitress came to see if there was anything that they needed Diane got up and rushed into the bathroom with her eyes shrouded in her hands. Keith sat at the table and waited for her to return. She never did. Here comes another phone call he thought.

Chapter 22

Joe O'Rourke was hardly paying attention to the television news as he waited for Diane to come home. The autotronic voices droned out the electronic information, which merely provided white noise for an otherwise quiet house.

As he flipped through the newspaper he considered putting on some music when it caught his attention. On the last page of the first section was a short news brief:

FAIRVIEW, ALASKA- One climber dead and two severely injured during failed attempt to summit Mt. McKinley. Park Service officials report that the surviving climbers were rescued in the midst of an arctic snow storm by Elaine Sutter of Port Angeles, Washington.

The death toll thus far this year on North America's highest peak has reached seven causing some to call for heightened safety regulations.

Joe set down the paper, turned off the television and sat in absolute quiet while he continued waiting for Diane. She was not that late and the pizza that had been delivered was in the oven keeping warm. He heard the lock clatter when she unlocked the door. He also heard her loud sigh as she laid her purse and briefcase on the kitchen counter.

"Hey, how was your day?"

"The usual, sorry I'm late. What do you want to do for dinner?"

"Got a pizza in the oven."

"Good, I didn't feel like going out."

Diane went to the bedroom to change into sweat pants and a T-shirt. She put Murine in her eyes in an effort to conceal the red. When she returned, Joe had the pizza out and portioned on two paper plates. He had also opened two cans of beer not bothering to pour the contents into glasses.

"You look tired." He handed her a plate and a beer.

"It's been a long week already. Do you love me?"

"Of course I do, why?"

"No, do you really love me no matter what?"

"I can't imagine what would make me not love you, what's going on?"

"I want to tell you something important for our relationship but I'm afraid it might ruin our relationship."

He set his beer down and sat back in his chair. "Spit it out, Diane."

"Before we went to Mexico, I had a one-night stand. It wasn't about anyone else and he means nothing to me." She pushed aside her plate. "I love you, Joe."

"With who?"

"It doesn't matter."

"The time you were gone all night?"

"Yes, before I came home and left again."

"I want to know who it was." His voice was serious but not combative.

"Do you promise not to do anything?"

"Sure."

"Keith Warren."

Joe got up and calmly walked over to her. He stood over where she sat and slowly emptied the contents of his beer can over her head. "You fucking whore."

"Joe … "

He did not stay in the house to listen to what she had to say. She followed him out and yelled for him to return. It was no use. He was gone.

Diane began frantically dialing all the numbers where she had to try to reach Keith. She got his answering machine at home and left a message without any regard to what his wife might think about some strange woman leaving a message for her husband. She tried his beeper and car phone.

154

It was not long before the phone began to ring. She picked it up hoping that it was Joe.

"Hi Diane, this is Keith."

"Keith I told Joe and he went ballistic. He's driving around somewhere. He may be looking for you."

"You told him about me? What did you tell him?"

"I told him about our little encounter. I didn't tell him that you have AIDS 'cause I'm not going to unless I have to."

"Then why did you tell him anything at all?"

"To lay the ground work in case I have to tell him more. Anyway, I don't want to keep secrets from him anymore."

"Shit, Diane, why … okay, then, thanks for the heads up." He hung up the phone.

Keith went into his confrontation mode. He was at home when he got the message and was careful to turn the ringers off on all of the phones in the house. He put blankets and a pillow on the couch in the family room pretending to watch a good movie. From his perch there he could monitor any cars pulling into the driveway or persons walking up to the door and preempt any direct assault upon the doorbell during the night. Finally, he ran over and over again in his mind that this was all Joe's fault until he had managed to fully convince himself that it was true. Keith was ready.

It was after two o'clock in the morning when Joe returned home. He walked into the bedroom and pulled the pillow out from under her head waking her.

"You're sleeping somewhere else." He threw her blankets on the floor outside the room.

"Joe … "

"Not tonight, just leave me alone."

Diane took the bedding and placed it on her couch without argument. Before she fell asleep, Joe walked back out into the dark kitchen and retrieved the newspaper from the trash can. He folded the front section in half and took it with him into the bedroom locking the door behind him.

Chapter 23

Climbing gear was still strewn about their little house. The rains had held off and June brought delightful weather to Port Angeles. They were glad to be back from Alaska and to have put their clients safely on a plane back to Chicago.

Hempstead and Elaine had been gone for three weeks and were sorting through their mail and retrieving phone messages in an effort to put together a business program for the remainder of the summer.

"Here's a couple that wants to do some easy hiking and rock climbing in Colorado for a week." She threw the letter in his direction.

"When?"

"Third week in July."

"Sounds good. I'd like to set a week aside and spend some time together without clients."

"What do you want to do?"

"I want to surprise you. Will you give me next week -- no questions?"

"What are you up to, Jim Hempstead?"

"Next week?"

"Why not?"

He went to see if there was any wine in the refrigerator. When he opened the door a foul odor hit with the punch of a bad smelling salt --some broccoli hidden in a storage drawer had spoiled while they were gone. Otherwise, it was empty. Elaine bargained to go to the store if Hempstead would clean it out.

But when she was gone he became drawn to the telephone. He walked over and picked it up listening blankly to the dial tone before pressing the numbers. 1-513-555-9775. It took a few seconds to connect and then it rang once before he hung it up.

Hempstead forced his concentration to the repugnant refrigerator in an effort to distract himself. He worked meticulously until it was sparkling clean. But the diversion didn't work--he couldn't escape from the vivid images of his son that were still tormenting him.

He sat down at the kitchen table and effortlessly scribbled down the words as they flowed easily through him. It didn't matter whether they were good, bad, sophomoric, or genius. He didn't care whether anyone else in the world would appreciate them. He was writing only for himself because it was how he felt. And seeing his thoughts solidified on paper only made it worse--it somehow validated his feelings, making them unbearable. He wadded up the paper in disgust and threw it toward the trash and then waited for Elaine.

They drank the wine and he told her all about it. She did her best to ease him back to their reality. But it wasn't going to work that night. Maybe some sleep, he thought, and he got up and went to bed.

Before she went to join him, Elaine found his crumpled up and unfinished note lying on the floor next to the trash can.

She read the following scrawled in Hempstead's messy hand:

The boy in the window
He waves to me,
My silent trip he spies,
Let me go,
Little boy in my window
He waves to me
He waves to me goodbye.

She neatly folded the note and placed it in a drawer. Coming to the bed, she bent down over him so that he could feel the warmth of her breath rushing into his ear as she spoke.

"Tell it that you will no longer let it take charge of you," she whispered.

He rolled over and looked into her eyes.

"You are in charge, Jim Hempstead. Take control." Her continued whisper did not disguise the command in her voice.

"I need you to be in charge," he said. "You are my talisman."

"I am with you always, Jim. So what do you have planned for next week?"

"I told you, it's a surprise."

"Tum de dum de dum … "

Chapter 24

Joe O'Rourke got up early the next morning, quickly dressed himself and left. His first stop was the public library where he sat alone for hours and looked through a stack of carefully selected books. Every once in a while he made notes on the tablet that he brought with him. When he was finished, he drove to the "Alpine Haus" where he sorted through climbing gear and talked at length to the help. He did not buy anything.

Diane did not go to work but she called Keith at the office.

"Did he come over last night?"

"No. He didn't call either. How is he?"

"I don't know. He came back and really didn't speak to me. He wasn't hostile. He left early this morning and didn't say a word."

"They all handle it differently."

"What?"

"Nothing. I'll let you know if I see or hear from him. Please try to get me if there is anything I need to know."

"He's acting strange and I'm never going to forgive you for this."

"Will you forgive yourself?"

She hung up the phone.

Chapter 25

The early-morning sun rising over the Sound cast brilliant orange and yellow hues upon the calm water. Hempstead had carefully loaded most of their gear into the two kayaks the day before and affixed them to the carrier on top of the Jeep. The smell of fresh fish wafted in from the docks as they stowed the rest of the equipment and left Port Angeles.

"This is going to be interesting, Where are we going?" she asked.

Hempstead produced a map of the San Juan Islands to show her at last. About eighty miles north of Seattle, the San Juan Islands are a cluster of approximately two hundred islands spread out between Anacortes, Washington and Vancouver Island, Canada.

Hempstead pointed on the map showing her that he planned for them to depart from a point on the northeastern coast of the Olympic Peninsula and spend several nights at state park camping sites on various islands until they reached Orcas Island. Their journey would not be unlike those of the native Indians who used these waters for trading routes long before they were discovered by Spanish and English sailors.

They drove for forty minutes or so east along the peninsula until he found the little dirt road leading to a small turn-out area hidden in the forest. The road to the water was narrow, rutted, and about a quarter mile long. There were two other cars parked at the conclusion in what had become a makeshift parking lot.

She helped him unload the kayaks and place them in the water. When the remainder of their gear was on board, Jim locked the Jeep and hid the keys under the gas flap.

Elaine climbed in her kayak without any questions as promised. She knelt in a sitting position and fastened the rubber skirt in place that prevented water from coming into the hold. When Hempstead was ready, they pushed off the dock and headed east careful to hug the coastline. The slight wind was enough to make the air smell and taste like salt.

It took them a little while to get accustomed to managing their paddles and vessels. Hempstead quickly developed abrasions on the backs of his thumbs from working the paddle. The minor discomfort, however, did not detract from his enjoyment of the moment. Indeed, he was delighted to be in the warmth and sun after three weeks in the snow and cold on Denali.

Elaine pulled up beside him. Her face was still wind-burned and tanned from the climb, except for the areas around her eyes where her goggles had sheltered her skin from the elements creating an odd raccoon-like appearance about her face.

"Are you sure we're going the right way?" she asked.

"It's my turn to lead … no questions, remember?"

"Just checking. Don't want to end up in Japan."

"Fuck you."

"Maybe tonight."

The kayaks glided easily across the glassy surface. Before long they heard the sound of air escaping from a purge valve followed by a loud clap of water. Not more than fifty yards in front of them was a pod of Orcas dancing in the water. They moved closer so that the spray cast from the blow holes sprinkled down upon them. Further out in front of the pod they spotted the sea lions that the whales were pursuing.

They ate lunch on a beach nestled inside a tiny and isolated cove. On either side of the beach there was a rocky outcrop that flowed from the forested shores and eventually jutted out into the water. After they ate they walked along the rocks and watched the freighters loafing by to the sea.

Back on the water the islands off in the distance appeared indistinguishable. They paddled lazily enjoying their time together. The sun that they had watched rise that morning was getting close to completing its path and began casting its orange and yellow colors off upon the water in the opposite direction that it had when the day had begun.

Elaine stopped and rested her paddle on the structure in front of her. "I don't think this is the way."

"It's my turn to lead, you promised. Besides, we've got all the supplies we need, we can camp anywhere."

"Your call, but I think that's San Juan Island over there." She pointed to a land mass about four miles away. "You're headed for Orcas Island."

"Can't be."

With that, they continued on with Hempstead leading the way and the sun quickly going down. They were still a mile or so away from whatever island Hempstead was leading them to when it became dark and dangerous. They put their headlamps on their heads and turned them on --hardly standard nautical running lights. Hempstead followed a course that seemed to be heading for a large complex on the island that was brilliantly lit up in the night.

When they arrived there were no private beaches or camp sites. They tied their kayaks up to the wooden dock in the marina and proceeded up the walkway.

Elaine looked up at the enormous mansion. "My god, I've never seen anything like this."

The Rosario hotel was built in the early 1900's by Robert Moran as his private mansion. Its walls were paneled in mahogany and its parquet floors were constructed with Indian teak. Since it became a hotel many years ago, the Rosario had become renowned for its palatial splendor in the wilderness.

Guests were enjoying drinks and the night out on the verandah. Soft music was coming from a pipe organ in the elegant music room that featured imported stained glass windows. In the foyer was a large wooden staircase leading up to the guest rooms.

"Can't believe I got us that far off course. Guess this will have to do for tonight." He reached for her hand as they walked up to the counter.

The gentleman in charge of the desk hardly looked up to greet them. "May I help you, please?"

"Got a room for the night? The name's Hempstead."

"Oh yes, Mr. Hempstead, we've been expecting you." An immediate change in attitude. "Will you still be staying for the week, sir?"

"Yes. Mind if I pay with cash?"

She squeezed his hand and abruptly jerked it down to her side. "You asshole," she whispered. "I love you."

Before they went up to their room, he reviewed the breakfast menu and placed an order for eggs benedict, hash browns, a pitcher of orange juice, english muffins, a pot of coffee, and champagne mimosas to be delivered no sooner than nine o'clock in the morning. "Thought we'd had enough of the wilderness for a while. You know, I still have a little bit of city left in me."

"I didn't even bring clothes for this kinda place."

"Don't think you're gonna need 'em."

She grabbed his arm again and led him to the staircase. "Tum de dum de dum ... "

Chapter 26

Diane was late coming home from work. She had to stop at the clinic to receive her negative test results. For the first time in days, she had some bit of good news and was starting to feel just a little better about things.

Joe was waiting at the kitchen table when she walked in. The lights were on and the stereo was playing loudly. In the center of the table was a large jug of cheap white wine that was about three glasses away from being full. His hair was a mess and he was wearing old gym shorts and a spotted T-shirt that looked like shit.

He pulled the chair next to him away from the table. "Sit down," he commanded.

Oh god, this is it, she thought. She had been waiting for days to see what his response would be because at this point his was the only one that mattered. She had mentally prepared herself for either outcome.

Diane did not think to remove her coat and took her seat in the awaiting chair. He reached for the jug and filled a glass that he had positioned in front of her.

"What's the matter, don't like my kind of wine?" he asked sarcastically.

"No, it's fine, Joe. I don't feel like wine right now."

"Drink the wine, goddammit. You drank his wine, you can drink mine."

She put the glass to her mouth and pretended to take a sip.

"Pretty good stuff, huh?"

"Yes, it's fine, Joe."

"We're gonna sit here and finish all of this wine and figure this out."

She rummaged around in her mind for a reason why she shouldn't just get up and leave. Why endure this? Because, of course, she deserved it. She stood again just long enough to remove her coat. This was going to be a long night.

"Do you love him?"

"No, I told..."

"Ah, you just fucked him, I get it."

"No, Joe, I..."

"Oh, so now you didn't fuck him?

"No, I told..."

"Can you just answer my question. Did you fuck Keith Warren?"

She took a real drink of the wine. "Yes, I had sex with him one time."

"Okay, so you fucked Keith Warren."

"If you say so."

"No, let's get this straight. You say so."

They both finished their wine and he filled the glasses again before setting the warming bottle back on the table between them.

"All right, I fucked Keith Warren, is that what you wanted me to say?"

"No, I never wanted you to say that. I never wanted you to ever say anything like it. I never even believed that it was possible that you might say something like that, let alone that I would want you to say that. You're the one that said it because you're the one that did it."

He swallowed all of the contents of his glass and pointed to her indicating she should do the same. When she did so, he filled their glasses again. Then he stood and turned away just long enough to wipe the tears from his cheeks.

"Do you want me to leave, Joe?"

"Why is this all of a sudden an issue about what I want? I didn't want to fuck Keith, you did. Were you thinking about what I wanted when you were fucking him? What do you want now, Diane?"

"I want this to have never happened. I'm sorry I hurt you."

He finished another glass and again signaled her to do the same.

"What do you want in regard to anything that you can do something about?" He refilled their glasses.

"I want us to take control of our lives again. I want to be with you, Joe. I understand I probably can't have that now."

"That's what I'm trying to figure out. We can't be anything unless we both want it. And I need to know that you want it before I can see if I can get over it."

"I understand. Take some time."

"No. No more time dammit. We're gonna figure this thing out right here and now….more wine?"

"What do you want me to do, Joe?"

"Tell me what is special between us now. Tell me what we have that exists only between us."

"Love."

"That's an easy word. We had love before you fucked Keith. I need to grasp onto something that remains special between us … something that has not been destroyed by this."

She put her hand on his arm. "Isn't it special that we both want this to work?"

"I don't know, Diane. I don't know." He stood again, filled their glasses and then walked to a cabinet. He opened the door, reached in and turned back to her. He was brandishing an ax-like object with a blade on one side and a lethal looking point on the other. He held it high in one hand for her to see. "This might make me feel better, Darling." He gritted his teeth together. "Don't you think this would make me feel better?"

Her heart was racing in terror. "Oh my god, Joe, no. Please, no."

He came towards her and she threw up her hands to cover her face. He slowly came around the table behind her and she sat waiting for it to happen. There was a loud thud as the ice ax hit the center of the table where it ended up lying next to the depleted jug of wine with its steely point rattling against the glass.

"I've thought about it, Diane. I want to do something with you that is special only to us. I need for that to happen if I'm gonna be able to make this work."

She sat dazed and perplexed by the drama unfolding in front of her. He pounded down another glass of wine.

"I want to do something with you that Keith Warren would never have done. I want to do something that belongs only to us."

"What are you talking about, Joe?"

"I want to go climb a mountain."

"Have you really ... "

"I've thought a lot about it, Diane. I want to climb a mountain with you. Nobody will be able to take that from us."

"I want to work this through, Joe, but we've never done anything like that."

"That's the point, goddammit!" His words were slurred.

She sat there for a good minute staring at the weapon in the middle of the table. Her punishment had just advanced into a warped dimension. "If you still want to do this thing in the morning, I'll do it. Where are we going?"

"I don't know yet. Haven't been able to get hold of the people. Will you do this for me?"

She picked up her glass and emptied it. "Yes."

Chapter 27

For two o'clock in the morning on an empty highway the asshole in the car behind him was following much too closely. Keith had spent the evening alone at the West End Tavern and only wanted to be left alone on his road home. He slowed down to let the car pull around him, but the car slowed with him. He changed lanes and so did the other car. He accelerated and changed lanes again. The phantom car remained with him.

He could see his tormentor in his rearview mirror swerving behind him and taunting him with flashing lights. He thought about calling 911 on his car phone, but then again he was not in a position to be talking to the police. The car pulled up next to him and started edging into Keith's lane. He pulled into the median to avoid a collision. In an effort to shake loose from his pursuer, he slammed on his breaks and could smell the smoke from his tires. Before stopping completely, he punched the accelerator again and still the other car rode along side of him in the chase for several more moments and swerved one more time in his direction to keep him in the median before it inexplicably sped away. Just at that instant, Keith's phone began to ring and his complete attention automatically went to it without hesitation.

He reached down for the receiver. "Hello." His voice was shaken.

There was nobody on the other end. He looked up again just in time to see the bridge's concrete pillar coming into his face.

It took them over two hours to pry what was left of Keith's tattered body from the ruins of his BMW. Dead on impact was the conclusion of at least one of the medics on the scene. It would have been hard for anyone to disagree. His face had gone through the steering wheel before it hit the windshield and then the concrete. The engine compartment had landed in what was left of his lap virtually severing his torso in half. They used dental records to confirm his identity because a visual would simply not be possible and there wasn't enough left of his fingers to rely upon prints.

The blood from his body tested at .187 for alcohol-- nearly twice the legal limit. Of course, there was no reason to test his blood to see whether it was tainted with anything else. Keith Warren had simply become another unfortunate drunk driving statistic.

When Diane heard about the news, she was more relieved that she would not have to deal with him again than she was concerned for his death. She did not bother to tell Joe. They had already buried Keith in the dirt of their lives and there was no good reason to dig up the bones.

Chapter 28

Their little house was a mess. In addition to the climbing gear left over from Denali, it now held out in the open the remnants of their kayaking trip--mostly unused equipment. The mail had collected itself in no logical pattern in small and scattered mounds about the kitchen table and counter area. If the weather people were right, it looked as though they had beaten the rains by a couple of days.

Jim was outside pulling the kayaks off of the Jeep, and she sat at the document-littered table wondering where to begin. It was almost July and they were scheduled to leave for Colorado in another week.

The phone rang and she answered it. "Adventure Travel." She listened for a few moments, then asked, "What'd you have in mind." ... "Oh, really." She reached for an envelope and pen to doodle and scribble down notes. "How much experience do you have?" ... "I don't think Denali is a good mountain for you. I'd suggest you start with something a little smaller." ... "Mt. Rainier is a good first climb." ... "About three days excluding travel time." ... "When did you have in mind?" ... "I don't think we have anything until the end of August." ... "For two people, that'd be five hundred dollars each, but I've gotta check with my partner. May I call you back?" She wrote down his name and telephone number on the back of the envelope.

Jim came in and dropped onto the couch. "It feels good to be home. Who was that?"

"Sometimes, I think we ought to call ourselves the 'Therapy Company.' A couple wants to climb a mountain -- it's going to shore-up their tattered relationship."

"What'd you tell them?"

"A psychologist would be safer."

170

He laughed. "No, really."

"I told them Rainier'd be a good first climb, but that I'd have to check with you. What do you think?"

"When?"

"Middle to end of August."

"Well, what do you think?"

"I don't know. July's the best time for Rainier. The crevasses start opening up by August. Gotta work your way around 'em."

"Rainier's pretty close by."

"That it is. I think we do it, and then leave right away for Jackson Hole. By September the summer tourists are gone and the skiers haven't arrived. The trees'll be changing color and it's a fantastic time to be there."

"You know how much I like Jackson. Shit, that's where I found you."

She picked up the envelope and called Joe O'Rourke. The Adventure Travel Company could accommodate his plan to climb a mountain, but it would have to wait until August. In the meantime, she strongly suggested that they work together to get in shape.

Chapter 29

Neither Diane nor Joe of them had been to Seattle before and August had brought remarkably clear weather to the Pacific Northwest. It was one of those rare days without clouds where they could see snow-covered Mt. Rainier looming over them imposing all of its glory from almost one hundred miles away. In fact, neither of them had really ever seen a mountain before and it was larger than either could have imagined.

Mt. Rainier's omni-present beauty often distracts from the fact that it is a volcano. Climbers near the summit can often smell a sulfur-like odor churning up from the center of the earth and lingering in the otherwise pristine air. The mountain is going to blow some day, it's only a question of when. And the mudflows and ashfalls that follow will surely devastate much of the Pacific Northwest and impact global weather patterns. For some, the notion of climbing an active volcano heightens the challenge and enhances the reward. Most people, however, live in blissful ignorance of the fiery charge held deep under its snowy cover. That certainly was the case with Diane and Joe.

Negotiating their way through the airport they maintained an upbeat humor even though the rental car company had mistakenly jettisoned their reservations into cyberspace. It took them over two hours to arrange for an alternate vehicle and begin following Elaine's directions to Paradise, where they intended to meet that night. When they were finally underway they resisted a playful impulse to drive north toward Seattle and investigate their locale. There would be time enough for that after the climb.

After that night of drunken madness when he first suggested that they embark upon this undertaking, Joe had

172

conceded to an uneasy and yet accepting connection with Diane. But now as they drove down the highway toward Mt. Rainier, he reached and placed his hand upon her knee as if to let her know they would be all right after all. His prescription for reconciliation appeared to be working as the spirit of their enterprise took them over.

It was twilight when they pulled into the massive parking area at the Paradise Inn. Behind and high above the cavernous lodge, the summit stood basking in what was left of the day's sunshine. Maybe Joe was right, she thought. If they could reach the top, they could accomplish anything.

Before checking into the hotel, he escorted her into the Glacier Lounge. It was full of little groups of people who had apparently assembled tables together to suit themselves and were having a good time. Diane and Joe drank a beer and eavesdropped on the climbing conversations going on all about them.

He lifted his glass to hers. "Thanks for doing this thing with me, Diane."

"Thank you, Joe. I've never seen anything like this place. It was a good idea." Sitting there in the lounge, she felt like the issues of their past were just that.

He finished his beer. "Better check in. We've got to meet Elaine in the restaurant in an hour."

The small wood-paneled room contained only two single beds, a desk, a bathroom, and a view of the mountain. When she came out of the shower she pushed him down on one of those little beds and made love to him for the first time since she had revealed her Keith Warren secret. This time, her passion did not arise out of a sense of duty or obligation. Indeed, she had not been such an eager participant for a long, long while. As Joe's laughter filled the little room, they saved just enough time to arrive at the restaurant as scheduled.

The hostess showed them to the table where Jim and Elaine were waiting. Both stood to greet them.

"Hi, Joe," Elaine shook his hand. "This is Jim."

"Nice to meet you. And this is Diane," he said, putting his hand on her shoulder.

"Well, let's sit down and have dinner." Elaine walked back to her position at the table.

Jim sent the waitress for a bottle of wine and they looked over the menus, which contained remarkably diverse and sophisticated selections for such a wilderness outpost.

Jim set down his menu. "So, what do you think of the Pacific Northwest?"

"It's unbelievably beautiful," Diane said. "I can't imagine that it's possible for us to climb Mt. Rainier."

Now Elaine set down her menu. "Anything's possible, Diane. I think you'll surprise yourself."

"Like I told you on the phone," Joe said, "we've never done anything like this."

"This is a good first mountain if you're in shape and you listen to us."

"I think we're in shape--we've worked hard in an effort to be anyway."

"Well," Elaine raised her glass to propose a toast, "to good mountains and making good friends."

Jim wondered whether he should say anything about the therapeutic aspect of this endeavor. He decided against it. After all, that was a personal issue.

It was a relaxed evening and Elaine went into detail about what would transpire over the next three days. She admonished them to get a good night's sleep and told them that they would all meet at the guide house at nine o'clock in the morning. That way Joe and Diane could rent necessary climbing gear. Joe didn't tell her that he already had an ice ax, but he did pick up the tab.

Back at their room, Jim opened the door for them. "I like those guys."

"Yea, so do I. Nice enough couple, and not ignorant enough to pretend they know what they're doing."

"There didn't seem to be any discord between them."

"I just told you what Joe told me."

174

"Well, if there is, it looks like they may be working it out."

"I love you, Jim."

"I love you, too, Princessa."

"Two weeks to Jackson Hole."

"Can't wait. Goodnight."

They spent the next day in the snow field above Paradise. Elaine gave them a primer on rope handling and glacier travel. For hours she had them practicing diving into self-arrest from every conceivable position. Over and over again they walked connected together up one side of a slope and down the other until it was automatic and they were not stepping all over the rope.

Even when they rested Elaine had them take off and put on their crampons until they could do it with their eyes closed. By the end of the day, Diane and Joe were worthy of a moderate route to the summit of Mt. Rainier. Even Diane thought to herself that it just might be possible after all.

Before walking back to Paradise, Elaine sat them down in the snow and told them about the climb. Leaving Paradise by ten o'clock in the morning, they would hike up to Camp Muir, where they would spend the night. The first day would not be technically difficult and would finish in a long steep climb up the Muir Snow Field. There was a primitive wooden hut at the camp where they would eat and try to sleep for about three or four hours before starting the technical climbing in the middle of the night up for the summit. The round trip to the top and back to Camp Muir would take about twelve hours or so, and then another two back down to Paradise. It was going to be a very long two days.

Chapter 30

They met at the guide house early in the morning. It had briefly rained the night before and the morning sun had already evaporated most of the residue. Everyone appeared rested and ready.

Elaine performed a final gear inspection before they started walking up the dirt path sprinkled with dead pine needles. Leaving Paradise, the grade was immediately and remarkably steep. The musty smell of wet foliage lingered in the forest. She did not drive them as hard as she had the day before when she was testing their stamina--today she was sparing it.

It was early afternoon when they reached Pebble Creek and the Muir Snow Field. This was a good place for lunch before they started up in the snow. Diane drank water from Joe's bottle while he searched his pack for the sandwiches that he had bought at the deli in Paradise that morning. They looked all about them and were thrilled to see the green Cascade Mountains still holding onto much of the snow left from the winter before. Maybe Joe was right, she thought again.

There was no need for an ice ax or crampons to ascend the snow field. They took a direct route using ski poles for balance. It was the end of August and they hadn't thought to put on gloves at this point. Both Diane and Joe wished they had, however. The higher they got up the snow the colder they became. They looked at each other and each knew that the other was suffering from the same condition. Even their exertion didn't keep their fingers from turning numb. But they also knew each other well enough to know that neither wanted to say anything for fear of raising a concern with their guides about their physical ability. So they just went on and hoped that it would get better.

Camp Muir was located at the top of the Muir Snow Field and the edge of the Cowlitz Glacier. There was a mobile-home sized tar shack that looked like a large wooden shoe box. Outside this "hut" was a wooden outhouse and up a little higher a more impressive looking stone structure where the rangers stayed. Just outside the front door was a wooden table set up on stilt-like legs so that people could use it to stand, eat and enjoy the view.

It was close to six o'clock at night when they arrived and walked into their accommodations for the evening. On the inside was another table with large plastic water coolers on it. In the rear was a large plywood sleeping area with a ladder ascending to another that was constructed like a bunk bed above it. There was a similar sleeping area built above the entrance. Against both walls was a long wooden bench built into the wall. Elaine told them that it was possible to "pack" over twenty people into this place. Tonight it would just be the four of them. Jim was glad that there would be some extra room. He hated sleeping in huts.

They were able to use the extra space to lay their gear out so that it would be ready in the morning. Jim boiled the water that they used to make their noodle-laden dinners. They stood outside at the table eating and watching the sun as it slowly lowered in the sky before them.

The sun had not yet completely set when Elaine suggested that they go into the hut and try to get some rest. They would be leaving shortly after midnight.

Elaine and Jim took the spot above the entrance for sleeping leaving Diane and Joe together at the other end of the hut. He nuzzled up against her and soaked up this private moment.

"Those guys really seem to be enjoying themselves," he whispered.

"I think this really was a good idea for them. I like her, but really don't have a read on him."

"I like both of them. Wish all of our clients were this easy."

They lay there quietly for a few more moments. It was apparent that she was on the verge of slumber. But there was no way he was going to sleep. Not only was this a hut, but the nondescript and omnipresent feeling of dread that he experienced for the first time going to Denali had taken him over again. He just lay there holding onto Elaine and waited for it to be time.

Under his breath he said, "I've given myself to you, Princessa."

She lightly threw back her elbow and hit him gently in the stomach in a playful gesture. "You're so dramatic, aren't you?"

He hadn't really thought she would hear him. It wasn't his intent. "Yea, so you've told me before," he said. "But you're the one that taught me everything I know."

"So you know I love you, too, Jim." She closed her eyes again and yawned "tum de dum de dum … "

Hempstead listened to the sounds the mountain was making in the darkness. The creaking from the slow movement of the glacier was occasionally interrupted by the thunder of building-sized chunks of ice releasing from their precarious holds and crashing down the mountain falling into little pieces before falling into the crevasses. The mountain felt very big to him that night.

At the other end of the small space, Diane and Joe were enduring their first night in a hut. They were both restless and concerned about their inability to fall asleep. Elaine should have told them that nobody really sleeps in these places so they might relax about it.

"I'm scared, Joe."

"That's what's going to make this worthwhile."

"Are you scared?"

"I don't know if 'scared' is the right word. I'm anxious, that's for sure."

"Do you think this is working? I hope you think so."

"I'm confident that after tomorrow you and I will enjoy an entirely new relationship."

It was a bright full moon that dominated a night sky unadulterated by clouds. There was very little wind and the temperature was somewhere in the mid-thirties. As Elaine put it, "this is the best I've ever seen it on Rainier."

They sat on the benches that lined the walls of the hut putting on clothing, drinking water, and consuming as much food as their altitude-stricken bodies would allow. One by one they walked outside to absorb the comfortable nocturnal beauty. Below them by about another thousand feet was a thick cloud layer that had every nook of its cottony texture revealed by the light of the moon. They were in an astounding world above the clouds and yet still four thousand feet from the summit.

When they were all outside, Elaine led them from the camp's rocky perch over a little headwall no more than two feet high and onto the Cowlitz Glacier. The moonlight reflected up off the snow and ice eliminating any need for artificial light.

Elaine lined them up against the uncoiled rope that she had already placed on the snow. She would be in the lead, followed by Joe, Diane, and then Jim on the end.

"Once we clip in, that's how we'll stay for the entire climb," she said.

"Do you mind if we switch so that I go behind Diane?" Joe asked. "I've always believed in ladies first."

"Look, Jim," she said, "we have a gentleman in our midst." They all laughed. "Sure, that's fine. You two just trade places."

After securing them onto the rope, Elaine checked to see that their crampons were fastened properly before clipping herself into the lead position. She would lead them across the glacier to a steep rocky-scree slope called Cathedral Rocks.

It was a relatively flat walk across the glacier as they weaved their way around the gapping crevasses that took a good eye to spot in the night. On several occasions Jim had to call out from behind and remind Joe to keep the slack out of the rope in front of him to avoid stepping on it. Other than that, the passage was uneventful and downright beautiful. After a good hour or so they were on the other side of the glacier and at the foot of the rocks.

Cathedral Rocks is a natural divider between the Cowlitz Glacier and the Ingraham Glacier, which they would follow the rest of the way to the top. They had to work their way up over the rocks cresting seven hundred feet from where they now stood.

It was a steep grade without snow and the sound of their metal crampons against the rock sounded like dozens of knives being slammed into stone. It was an unnatural and unnerving noise. And whenever one of their feet would slip, the skidding metal against rock would cause sparks to fly in the night. None of them was disappointed when they were back on the snow on the other side.

On the Ingraham Glacier, they walked for a little while along a level plateau until Elaine announced that they had reached their first rest area. They sat connected by their rope and huddled in a semi-circle putting on parkas to keep the warm during the respite. It was still dark, which was good because the sun had not yet been able to warm the snow and ice formations up ahead. They were about to go through a massive icefall, which is the site of the worst mountaineering accident in North American history.

Gigantic blocks of ice the size of buildings could be broken loose at any moment by the glacier's natural flow or just enough sun to melt away their temporary fixtures. Not too many years ago a large serac came down, spraying out large blocks of ice upon a group of climbers and sweeping eleven of them into a crevasse never to be found. If the ice toppled while they were passing through, there really wasn't much of anything they could do about it.

Except Joe, they snacked, drank and fidgeted with their gear. He just sat playing with the rope lying between his legs and playing with his pocketknife. Elaine told them that once they started again, they would move quickly and without stopping until they were through the ice fall. After hearing about it, they all pretty much agreed with that strategy.

Elaine measurably picked up the pace when they were moving again. The level snow they had been on soon gave way to a narrow catwalk with a massive crevasse dropping to one side and the unknown of the ice fall rising to the other. Their clients' steps were noticeably hesitant.

She got them safely through the icefall and to the base of Disappointment Cleaver. The sun was coming up giving them their first opportunity to take in the mountainous contours all around them. They could look back and to the west and see a notch between Cathedral Rocks and the massive Gibralter Rock called "Cadaver Gap." It got its name in 1929 from the rescuers who evacuated the bodies of two climbers over it and down to Camp Muir. Like so many others, Hempstead believed that Cadaver Gap was appropriately named by the people with the prerogative to do so: after all, it wasn't like they were picking out the name for some cozy street in the suburbs. To the east the black outline of Little Tahoma peak stood in sharp contrast to the rapidly brightening sky.

They stood panting at the bottom of the steep rock and snow incline that was about four or five hundred feet in length. For inexperienced climbers, Diane and Joe were climbing strong and Elaine allowed a brief opportunity for them to collect themselves before moving on.

Ascending Disappointment Cleaver proved to be a little dicey for them, just as it had for so many other climbers before them. Without a lot of experience, their clients' climbing got sloppy as things got difficult. At one point Joe caught his crampons on the rope tripping him to his knees. Jim dove into self-arrest, although it was unnecessary because Joe was able to catch himself. At another point when Joe stepped on the rope again it jerked Diane, pulling her off balance and causing her to fall like a domino backwards into Joe and then Jim. That time it was Elaine who went into self-arrest keeping them from falling back into the icefall.

After about forty minutes they were on top of the cleaver and Elaine signaled that it was time for them to rest again.

"How're you guys feeling?" she asked.

"Pretty good," Joe answered. "I had a little trouble back there, but this is fantastic."

"You're right, Joe, you need to be a little more careful about the rope," Jim said. If he hadn't liked them so much, he would have been much sterner. Anyway, he was certain that he had gotten his message across.

Diane was clearly elated with the climb and asked how much further they had to go. It was not a question raised out of a concern for the distance but instead out of a desire to savor the adventure--she didn't want it to end. Elaine told her it would be about three more hours, but that they had just come up the most difficult part. Pulling her aside as much as was possible connected to the rope, Diane quietly asked her how to go about relieving herself.

Elaine laughed. "Eyes forward, men. Diane and I have some business to take care of behind you."

Diane was embarrassed and hesitant at first, but her physical needs won out over her social concerns. She joined Elaine a couple paces above and behind where the men were sitting.

Jim leaned over to Joe while they were waiting and said "mountains can humble a person in many ways." They both laughed.

The sun was completely out now, and they were all very warm. Far below them the clouds still lingered blocking off any view below Camp Muir. They had not run across any other climbers and appeared to have the mountain to themselves.

Soon it was time for them to move again. They advanced up and around a series of deep crevasses creating a fresh switch-back trail in the snow. Altitude was increasingly becoming a factor for Joe and Diane but they were ahead of schedule so Elaine slowed her pace to accommodate them. It would also help them conserve energy for the mandatory descent from the top. Jim was somewhat relieved with the slowed progress. He had thought that Rainier would be an easy walk in the snow after Denali and was surprised at how wasted he was becoming. Kick, rest, step. Kick, rest, step.

Mt. Rainier is capable of dishing out devastating weather conditions, but not today. In the warmth of the summer sun they were working their way up and over a series of seemingly endless rises. They were exhausted but remained fortified by Elaine's incessant encouragement. It didn't look like they had that much farther to go, but then again it had appeared that way for hours. The truth was that they were about at the point where the Ingraham Glacier merges with the Emmons Glacier below the summit crater.

Coming up over one of those rises Diane found Elaine standing and waiting with nowhere left to climb. There was no other feeling like it. Together, she and Joe had just accomplished what had seemed the impossible.

"Thank you, Elaine, with all of my heart," she said waiting for Joe to come to her. There was no other way for her to describe how she felt at that moment.

Elaine turned and left them alone. They embraced and held onto each other for a good minute.

She removed a hand to wipe away her tears. "Oh God, Joe, isn't this beautiful?"

"We did it. I can't believe we made it."

On top of the world they could see the jets flying below them in route between Portland and Seattle. Far off in the distance they could also see the snowy peak of Mt. Hood in Oregon, and what remained of Mt. St. Helens. After some private time, Elaine offered to take them across the crater to sign the summit register and look down upon Seattle.

Diane held out the camera that she had been wearing around her neck. "Would you please take a picture of us first?"

They posed there on the summit with their arms around each other's waist. With their other outstretched arms they held their ice axes up high in victory and smiled for the camera. After the picture, Elaine led them to the other side of the crater where they signed the register provided by the park service preserving their achievement in the public record forever.

"This is one of those rare days that guides live for," Elaine said. "This makes it all worthwhile." She allowed more than the usual half hour on the summit before telling them it was time to go.

They started walking down the mountain in the same order that they had climbed up. Joe and Diane promptly learned that going downhill in the snow can be more difficult than going up. The sun had warmed the snow so that it was balling up in their crampons. Elaine showed them how to knock the snow out with their axes before every step so that the points would be exposed enough to grip the glacier. It was a technique they had never practiced before.

They moved tentatively and were forced to go into self-arrest on several occasions because either Diane or Joe would fall when their feet would skid out from under them. This was not unusual and would simply require a little more time for them to reach Camp Muir.

Before long they came to a place where the slope below them dropped completely out of view only to emerge again at the mouth of a crevasse. They really needed to be careful here because there wasn't much room for error. With only one of them walking at a time, they each took their turn moving until the rope pulled the person behind them into motion.

Watching from behind, it almost looked to Jim as if Joe intentionally reached over and stepped on the slack in the rope beside him. Whether it was intentional or not, when he caught the rope it pulled Diane off balance causing her to fall like a rock down the slick and steep slope. Neither she nor Joe screamed and by the time Jim called out it was too late to alert Elaine to the debacle occurring behind her. She joined Diane in the free fall as Jim dove into self-arrest.

At the same time that the rope pulled tight it pulled Joe off of his feet before breaking in the location that he had stepped on it. Looking back between his legs from his self-arrest position, Jim watched in horror as Elaine and Diane sailed off tied together down the mountain and out of sight into the gaping abyss just below where they were descending. The last thing he saw was them tumbling together in a swirl of crampons and rope with their limbs bending and twisting in directions that nature had never intended. Only one of them was screaming, but he couldn't tell which one of them it was. Joe followed them almost simultaneously into the opening still tethered by the rope to Jim.

It all happened so quickly. Too many thoughts came rushing into his mind at the same moment for any one of them to be intelligible. He had lost Elaine. He had Joe's life in his hands. Had he just seen Joe step on the rope and try to kill Diane and Elaine? What should he do now? His body began shaking uncontrollably and he didn't know whether the raw emotion that he felt at that moment was an urge to scream, cry, or both.

He wanted to go look into the crevasse for Elaine but he couldn't move from the stance that was securing him and Joe. He was trapped in self-arrest with Elaine's murderer alive and hanging at the end of the rope. That's why Joe was stepping on the rope all day long, he thought. This was all planned. For the entire day Jim had witnessed murder in progress and hadn't done a damn thing to stop it.

Wait a minute, he thought. You're a lawyer. You know better than to assume things. You can't simply jump to the bizarre conclusion that this was murder. You know better than to act as judge and jury. You're panicked and thinking like a crazy person. This was probably a freak accident.

Whatever it was he needed to get to Elaine but he was trapped. He could hear Joe yelling from inside the crevasse, but couldn't understand what he was saying. Elaine's going to come up over the ledge and tell him what to do. He just needed to give her some time.

Joe was getting heavy on the end of the rope and Jim's calf muscles started to painfully cramp. There was no way for him to move to ease them or even get some water to drink. Come on, Elaine, hurry up, he thought.

He didn't know how long he'd stayed there in that awkward position when the sun rapidly started to go down. He had become familiar with each of the thousands of snow crystals that had been staring him in the face for hours and it was driving him mad. Why was he staying there saving a murderer? Because he's not a murderer, and you're just imagining things. It's your obligation as a guide to save your client. It's your obligation as a lawyer to let the justice system decide whether this was murder. It's your obligation to Elaine to drop this fucker. No, then you'd be just as bad as he. Anyway, this was just a fateful mishap. Hurry up, Elaine.

It was turning dark and he was getting cold. Clouds had blown in from the West and there was very little light for him to see. Jim's body was quickly giving way and his mind was long gone. If he didn't do something soon, he would end up joining them all in the crevasse. He hadn't heard anything from Joe in a long while. Maybe he was dead and this was all a wasted effort. This is stupid, he thought. You've been standing here for hours holding onto a dead body--a dead murdering body.

He felt the relief caused by the instantaneous absence of Joe's weight. No decision that he had ever made in his life had such immediate and irrevocable consequences. The moment he cut the rope he wanted the option to put it back together again. There wasn't one. Folding up the knife and putting it back in his pocket he felt his life coursing out of control again.

He stood on the precipice and stared into the blackness of the bottomless crevasse for the longest time. He couldn't see or hear a thing. Elaine was alive, he reasoned, so he needed to go get help. Leaving his pack lying in the darkened snow, he began scrambling down the mountain toward Camp Muir where someone could radio and get help for Elaine.

Chapter 31

Jim Hempstead spent the next several days at the Paradise Inn refusing to talk to anyone. He existed in a trance and confined his movements to his room and the bar. The officials in charge of the investigation had decided to let him speak when he was able. Until then, there was no urgency because life was no longer at stake. The search and rescue teams had found only a camera and an ice ax. Among themselves, they had given up any hope of retrieving the bodies. The crevasse was simply too large and complex. They would keep looking, though, because it was still too soon to give up their token optimism.

Like the night before, Hempstead had gone to his room to try to sleep only after he had obliterated himself with alcohol. It was the only prospect that he had for calming the racing mind that was forbidding him rest.

Sometime in the middle of the night a man pounded loudly on his door. "Wake up, Jim!" he shouted and pounded some more.

Hempstead finally struggled to his feet and stammered to the door to let him in.

"We've found Elaine," the man said with great excitement, "and she's alive!"

"What? Where is she?" he asked. "Where is she, goddammit?"

"Calm down, man. They've got her in a chopper headed to Seattle."

"Why ... get me to Seattle ... can I speak with her?"

"She made it, Jim. She made it."

"What the fuck is going on? Tell me what's going on."

Elaine had come to in excruciating pain and completely disoriented. Her arm ached and her head pounded miserably. She was still connected to Diane, who was crumpled in a heap next to her in the blood-stained snow. She knew immediately that her arm was broken and was pretty well convinced that she was suffering from at least a concussion. Her bladder had emptied creating a chilling sensation about her waist and yet her immediate reaction was to inspect the scene looking for Jim. She did not give any regard to her fortunate survival as her heart sank in the realization that he was nowhere to be found.

Elaine and Diane had landed in the bowels of a massive crevasse and there was no way for her to judge how far down they were. Elaine supposed the worst for Diane, but checked anyway. Her suspicion was correct so she unclipped herself with her good hand and discarded the fragment of useless rope that remained.

There was no food or water and she presumed that the sun must be setting because the deep-blue reflection from the massive ice structure was quickly fading into gray. She was not ready to die, and if she sat helplessly in this crack in the ground she certainly would. Before she could move, however, everything suddenly went to black.

It was cold when her awareness came back to her. She had no idea how long she had been out, but it was light again. To avoid hypothermia, she salvaged clothing from Diane's body and then rummaged though her backpack for something to drink. Nothing. She did not expect to be rescued or that anyone even knew where she was. It was either time to move or to give up.

The pain in her arm remained incredible and only got worse each time it moved as it dangled to her side. She cut a three-foot section from the rope remnant and threw it around her back. Reaching behind her, she pulled the rope back in front so that it was wrapped around her body securing her damaged arm to her torso. It took several tries for her to tie a knot with one hand sufficient enough to keep the rope brace in place. Then she checked to see that her crampons were secure.

The rush of blood pumping to her head as she stood nearly sent her back down. She let her dizziness subside before she kicked her first step into the icy wall. The vibration rattled through her aching arm and head. She sunk her ice ax in above her head and held on as she kicked a higher step with her other foot. This first movement in a slow escape progress committed her to the task. Without a rope, if she passed out again, she would fall unconsciously to her death.

It was questionable whether her determination could overcome the pain, hunger, and exhaustion. Elaine worked for what seemed like hours for a mere thirty feet of progress. She felt the beginning of the ominous vertigo that signaled approaching unconsciousness. Having no choice, she was able to screw an anchor into the ice and clip the carabiner dangling from her harness onto it before she passed out again.

This time when awareness came back to her, it was dark and she was hanging by her waist to the wall of the crevasse. Again, there was no telling how long she had been there. It was not possible for her to search her pack for a headlamp so she unclipped from the safety of the anchor and resumed her escape in the dark.

She climbed until her legs and working arm throbbed from the excessive build-up of lactic acid. She eventually came to a ledge that was probably no more than four feet at its widest point but it was a good place to rest until it was light again. The hunger and cold did not bother her as much as the thirst. Her tongue was swollen and felt like it was stuck to the roof of her mouth. Her lips were cracked and bleeding. She broke the horrible silence by talking aloud to herself. The echoes from her voice ricocheted throughout the cavern and disappeared.

She struggled to stay awake until the first light came. She had to move again to chase away the chill even though every part of her body hurt until the endorphins started working. By now, the familiar blue environment had begun playing games with her mind. Until her forced concentration melted them away, she was seeing faces in the crystal--none more clearly than Jim's.

A single snow flake floated down and landed on her mitten. It was followed shortly by more until it seemed to be raining large white confetti. She knew she must be close to the opening and began screaming for Jim. There was no response as the shouts reverberated about her. Looking up, she could see the precipice that she had fallen over and which now marked the location of Diane's tomb. Elaine became invigorated with the knowledge that she would not die in the crevasse. In twenty more minutes she would emerge from this hole in the ground that she had come to know so well.

When she came up over the crease and onto the glacier the wind was blowing so hard that she did not risk standing and getting blown off the mountain. She lay face down in the snow with the blizzard blasting over her and longed in some demented manner to be back within the safety of her crevasse.

She had come too far to give up now. Elaine struggled to remove a crampon and began using the points to dig a shallow shelter in the snow. When it was just deep enough, she laid down and covered as much of her body with the excavated snow as possible. The cocoon helped with the wind but not with the cold. There was nothing left for her to do but wait out the storm. She worked hard to stay awake because she understood that when people freeze to death they often feel like they are simply going to sleep. She thought about all the things she wanted to do with Jim and their life when this was over. She recited her limerick over and over again and tried to think of all the words that rhymed with rain.

She shivered in the night and listened to the wind that sounded like a thousand ghosts from hell howling out in their agony. Then she saw a small break in the clouds and the sparkling ladle of the Big Dipper. The snow and wind eased as the storm began to break. The temperature dropped as the little heat that the clouds had managed to hold close to the earth was now able to escape into space.

Elaine's only goal was to make it through the remainder of the night but it was too cold to lie there. She drew up her knees and kicked the snow off her. She would take her chances working her way back down to Camp Muir by the little light provided by the stars.

It took her some time to locate the crampon she had removed earlier that night in the midst of the storm. Strapping it back onto her foot with only one mitten-encumbered hand was impossible. She bit one end of her mitten and pulled it off into her mouth exposing her hand to the cold. By doing so, she could manipulate the straps to secure the crampon in place. When she slid her hand back into the mitten her fingers felt like they were being run through a meat grinder as the blood attempted to circulate again. She opened and closed her fingers and then squeezed them into her palm in an effort to expedite the return of her warm blood supply. Her nose and cheeks were already numb from frostbite.

When she stood she became dizzy and staggered in place for a moment. She did not take more than ten steps down the mountain before she fell and landed on her injured arm screaming out in pain. Rising to her feet again, Elaine struggled down the mountain oblivious to any concern for the hundreds of crevasse openings that lined the way back to Camp Muir.

The first rays of the sun turned the snow orange. Elaine dropped to her knees and scooped up a handful of snow in her mitten and tried to eat it. It did not satisfy her thirst and instead froze her tongue and caused her to begin shivering again. As she sat there in the snow she spotted a chain of headlamps coming up the mountain from about five hundred feet below her. She did not have the energy left to go to them, but she was not about to leave it to fate that they would happen upon her. Stammering to her feet, Elaine headed off in the direction of the headlamps.

The climbers had left Camp Muir at about one o'clock in the morning and were resting at the second of their planned stops in route to the summit. There were three rope teams of four climbers per team in addition to a guide. They were drinking water and taking pictures of the sun coming up over Little Tahoma peak.

"Holy shit." One of them saw her staggering down the mountain, falling, getting up, and then falling into their midst. "Get over here!" he called to one of the guides.

The guide came over and rolled Elaine over onto her back. "My God," he said. "Can you hear me?"

"Please give me some water." Her voice was hushed and dry.

"Somebody throw me a water bottle!"

It landed near his feet. He picked it up and slowly poured its contents into her mouth. When she was able to hold it by herself, he went to get his sleeping bag to wrap around her.

"What happened? Are there any others?"

She muttered something incomprehensibly before letting out a groan and passing out again.

Jim Hempstead imagined it all. He thought about how utterly alone she must have felt. He hoped that the break did not pierce her flesh and cause infection. He wondered whether she would lose the arm. He lived her struggle to stay awake and moving. He thought about her in pain while he was safe and warm at Paradise.

After quickly dressing himself, Hempstead drove three hours in the night back to Seattle and found his way to Swiss Hospital. Her floor was quiet and the night nurse led him to her room. Elaine was asleep with her bandaged hands lying above the covers on her stomach. The I-V line was slowly dripping its fluid into her and he pulled up a chair next to the beeping heart monitor. All he wanted was to wake her and let her know he was there and grateful to still have her in his life. He wanted to talk about how gorgeous Jackson was going to be. He reached over and lay one of his hands on hers and sat there waiting until he eventually fell asleep in his chair.

****

Jim Hempstead opened his eyes and in that terrible instant realized that he had been dreaming. He was lying in his bed in Paradise and nowhere near a hospital in Seattle. The sobering awareness was overwhelming. He was alone in his dark room and Elaine was dead in a crevasse. He ached for her and wanted nothing else other than to wake up again to his dream. No. Maybe this was his dream. Oh, God, he thought, please let this be my dream.

He got up and dressed himself but he did not go to the bar. Instead, he passed it by and walked outside for the first time since he had come off the mountain. He left Paradise and began hiking in the night up the trail to Pebble Creek and the snow field that leads back up the mountain. He did not feel the cool rain as it fell upon him.

Hempstead had finally collided irreconcilably with his past. He wondered where she was. Her spirit and life began to fill him and yet he was completely alone. He thought about what she would say if she could speak to him. Would she tell him that death is just the other side of life? That's bullshit. There would be no life without her.

He walked onto the snow field looking up toward the direction of the glacier. "Princessa!" he shouted with all his might. He continued shouting until his voice could not handle any more. Then he shouted again.

He wept as he headed back over to a group of rocks that stood beside the snow field. He knew that it would not take long once he began to bleed. A calm came over him as the angst flowed from his body with the blood.

He heard the hushed voice come to him. "I love you, Jim Hempstead," and he felt her lay his head back in her arms and comfort him. "It'll be all right."

"Elaine?" he forced a whisper from his mouth. He was not certain whether he was dreaming, dead or alive. He didn't care. He was certain that he was in her presence and that was all he had ever wanted. "It's raining, Elaine."

She rocked him in her arms. "I know."

Joseph and Diane O'Rourke were laid together for eternity. Next to their graves was a poster-size photograph of them holding each other on the summit of their mountain. It was a wonderfully beautiful autumn day that did not notice or care for the sorrow shared by those who came to grieve. Those persons would never know of the events that had brought them to that place.

A thousand miles away there was a chill in the air. Jackson had been deserted for the fall and the trees had already changed color casting a brilliant golden blanket upon the valley floor.

And just north of town, in the wilderness that lies beyond Colter Bay, someone had built a fire in a little cabin that sits on the edge of a lake.

*** *

194